DEATH IN THE DARK

Longarm dove forward into the tricky light of the windowless hallway. He was glad he'd come in fast and low when another gun blazed in the gloom down the hall to envelop him in black-powder smoke and repeated ear-splitting roars as he belly-flopped to the floor and fired back with his Winchester until he heard somebody yell, "I give up! I give up! You got me bad and I need me a doc!"

Longarm fired at the sound of the other cuss on the floor, and grunted in satisfaction as he heard somebody scream like a coyote giving birth to a litter of busted bottles. . . .

DON'T MISS THESE
ALL-ACTION WESTERN SERIES
FROM THE BERKLEY PUBLISHING GROUP

TABOR EVANS

LONGARM

AND THE
BARBED WIRE BULLIES

JOVE BOOKS, NEW YORK

LONGARM AND THE BARBED WIRE BULLIES

A Jove Book / published by arrangement with
the author

PRINTING HISTORY
Jove edition / October 1994

All rights reserved.
Copyright © 1994 by Jove Publications, Inc.
This book may not be reproduced in whole
or in part, by mimeograph or any other means,
without permission. For information address:
The Berkley Publishing Group, 200 Madison Avenue,
New York, New York 10016.

ISBN: 0-515-11476-6

A JOVE BOOK®
Jove Books are published by The Berkley Publishing Group,
200 Madison Avenue, New York, New York 10016.
JOVE and the "J" design are trademarks
belonging to Jove Publications, Inc.

PRINTED IN THE UNITED STATES OF AMERICA

10 9 8 7 6 5 4 3 2 1

Chapter 1

It was April Fool's Day. But Deputy U.S. Marshal Custis Long of the Denver District Court hadn't suspected the old-timers out back of Wallington & Murphy's Dry Goods were funning him when they'd as much as promised a blizzard by nightfall, no matter what the calendar said. The brisk morning breezes off the Front Range had tasted like snow, and by noon the sky had commenced to look a lot like the bottom of a big old galvanized washtub.

But come fair weather or foul, an old pal from his trail-herding days had called for help in writing. So Longarm, as he was as often called by friend and foe alike, was on his way with a quarter ton of help in the bed of his hired box wagon. He was dressed for the chore in old denim work duds, instead of that infernal suit the current Administration expected him to wear around his home office in the Denver Federal Building.

He'd hired a team of retired army mules, at a good price, off a livery near the dry goods outfit. They knew better than to cheat a lawman who'd be back in town, and had understood he was only fixing to haul a quarter ton less than forty miles. The team hadn't given him any sass along the tree-lined back

1

streets of town. But once they were out on the old post road to the southeast, with those breezes just a tad more brisk, the two critters had commenced to take on like librarian gals spooked by mice every time the winds rolled a tumbleweed along the dusty wagon trace. Thanks to the time of the year, and the more reasonable spring rains they'd been having of late, there wasn't much dust, save for what they were kicking up themselves as they trotted along at an easy but mile-eating pace. The rolling short-grass prairie all around was as green as it usually got, with the prickle poppies and pasqueflowers in bud. Every furlong or so, a yucca-like soap-weed was poking up what looked like a giant asparagus spear that was fixing to burst into cascades of waxy white flowers by May—if everything didn't get frozen back to the root crowns.

Heading out into an uncertain situation on some of his stored-up vacation time, Longarm had naturally draped his McClellan saddle and personal possibles over the backrest of the wagon seat. So he was able to rustle up the sheepskin mackinaw he'd been smart enough to bring along without having to rein in. It wasn't cold enough for a man who admired fresh air to button up yet. But as he shrugged it on over his summer-weight denim jacket, he felt a heap better about that wind at his back. The mules had him and the wagon box between the raw westerlies and their bare brown rumps, so what the hell.

Something cold and wet lit on the nape of his neck. He hoped it was rain. Then he commenced to spy small white flakes flying by and protested, "Aw, come on, Lord. It's too late in the greenup for any more damned snow!"

The Lord didn't answer directly. Longarm knew what he'd just said was a white lie. Those geography-book writers who warned that the climate of the High Plains west of Latitude 100 could best be described as "treacherous" had doubtless been out this way a time or two. It was almost as easy to die of heatstroke in March as it was to freeze to death in June, with nothing out here to slow the wind worth mentioning.

As they topped a gentle rise, the wind hit hard enough to sway the loaded box wagon under Longarm. The snow was starting to stick to the green grass in the draw beyond. A plainsman with a lick of sense meeting up with a late-spring blizzard this close to town would be turning back, and Longarm had become quite a sensible plainsman since heading out this way from West-by-God-Virginia after the war. But what the hell, the wind was to his back instead of slapping him in the face.

The air lay more still, with the snow falling thicker, as he drove across the wide shallow draw. Then it was back up into that infernal wind, blowing harder now, which peppered his exposed hide good with snow frozen almost as hard and sharp as ground glass.

But that was why "cowboys" and other High Plains riders wore the bandannas those Eastern folks found so "colorful." The shoestring tie President Hayes expected a federal lawman to wear when he was on duty these days wouldn't have done a whole lot for Longarm just now. But his good old calico bandanna, looped over his telescoped brown Stetson and tied under his chin, with the collar of his mackinaw all the way up, had him snug as a bug in no time. It was a good thing there wasn't another living soul within miles to see how dumb he looked.

He buttoned up the front while he was at it, deciding not to be silly about the .44–40 riding cross-draw on his left hip and out of handy reach at the moment. For there wasn't anything dangerous as a carrion crow out and about in this gathering storm, and in any pinch, he had the walnut stock of his Winchester saddle gun sticking up into the gray sky beside him as he drove on, and on, and then on some more, singing above the moan of the winds:

3

"But we poor unfortunates live in a clime
That calls for at least three full suits at a time,
A thick one and thin one, for days cold or hot,
And a medium-weight, for the days that are not!"

It was just as well he was down in another draw when he paused between verses. For he'd have had a time making out that distant cry if he'd been singing in the wind on top of the rise beyond. It was tough enough to be certain he'd really heard it as it was. Winds and lonesome ears played all sorts of tricks in the great outdoors. He'd wasted a heap of sympathy and considerable effort on that first mountain lion he'd ever heard, trying to save what he'd taken for a lost child in the foothills late at night. A jackrabbit hung up in a drift fence could also sound a lot like some kid in need of help. But then he heard that distant wail again, and stood up to yell back, "Where are you at and what's busted?"

He couldn't make out the words, but that had to be some female yelling into the wind at him from along the post road a piece. She'd doubtless been able to make out his words better as the wind blew them in her face. So he called out some encouragement and just drove on. Then sure enough, one of those two dark blurs in the swirling snowfall ahead seemed to be waving like hell at him.

As he drove down into the shallow draw the wind died some more and he could make out: "Thank heavens someone heard me! I don't know why my poor horse just staggered off the road and fell out from under me like that. But he did, over an hour ago, and I'm *freezing* out here in this ridiculous weather!"

Longarm said he could see that as he set the brake and got down to take off his mackinaw and wrap it around the skinny little thing in a fashionable riding habit of chocolate-brown

4

serge. She leaned into him, sobbing, "Oh, Lord, that feels so good. I must not have known how cold it had gotten since I rode out of Aurora no more than two hours ago! But what about *you*, good sir?"

To which Longarm replied, "I ain't no sir, ma'am. I'm Deputy U.S. Marshal Custis Long, and before that I drove cows in worse weather than this in shirtsleeves. You're right about how ridiculous the weather can act betwixt dead winter and high summer out our way. You say your mount just up and foundered on you, ma'am?"

She let go of him. "My friends call me Cindy, albeit it's Miss Lucinda Fuller if you want to be formal, ah, Custis."

He said, "I'd best see what's wrong with your mount, Miss Cindy." Then he moved around her to get at the chestnut gelding playing bear rug in the snow-frosted grass just off the wagon trace. The falling snow wasn't stuck to the brute's hide yet, but the sidesaddle was already commencing to look as if it had been dusted with flour to bake to a crisp. Intense cold had about the same effect as intense heat on both leather and untanned living hide.

First things coming first, Longarm saw the foundered mount knew what he was doing and didn't cotton to it, judging by the feeble way it tried to bite him. When he saw that handy near hind leg behaving so peaceful, he took hold, digging a thumb into the swollen member, and ducking as the poor brute tried in vain to take his head off with a fore-hoof. Then he rose back to his own considerable height and drew his exposed six-gun as he told the gal wrapped in his big mackinaw, "He's spavined, bad, ma'am. Are you saying you didn't know your own mount was spavined when you started out to wherever this morning?"

She replied uncertainly, "He's not my personal property. I hired him, along with that saddle, from a well-recommended livery back in Aurora. I told them I had to get over to my

5

sister's homestead near Kiowa, and they assured me this was a reliable old trail mount."

"They lied," Longarm said. "I don't know who recommended the outfit, but I mean to have a talk with the skunks on my way back. It wouldn't be proper for me to tell a lady what I mean to say to anyone who'd send even a man out on a forty-mile ride aboard a spavined mount!"

She confessed in a small shy voice that she wasn't sure just what he meant. So he said, "Spavin is a disease of riding stock a mite like the rheumatiz is to us, Miss Cindy. It settles mostly in the critter's hocks, which look like backwards knees but would be ankles on a human limb. It's called bone spavin when the joint fills up with chalk, and bog spavin when it swells with goo. In either case this poor old cuss ain't never going to get better, and ought to be put out of his misery, with your permission, of course."

The gal sobbed, "Can't you do anything for him? They're expecting me at my sister's, and it's too far to walk back to Aurora even if I *wanted* to!"

Longarm said, "You'd never make it in this weather. I just told you there was nothing anyone could do about a spavined mount but gun it. As to getting you and your saddlebags somewhat closer to Kiowa, Miss Cindy, I'd be proud to give you a wagon ride as far as the Wade spread a few miles short. I'm sure my old pal Jeff Wade would be proud to lend you another pony, once you've been warmed up and fed an early supper."

She clapped her bare hands in delight and called him a life-saver. So he led her over by the wagon, and told her not to watch as he went back to gun her spavined livery nag.

She screamed anyway. So did one of the mules, and it was a good thing he'd set the wheel brakes. Lots of critters were spooked by the dulcet tones of a .44-40. Longarm, like many another rider in such an uncertain old world, favored rounds with twice the kick and far more range than the standard army .45-28 because you could load both your six-gun and Winchester with the same brass as long as you didn't mind a little noise.

Having blown out the foundered chestnut's brains, Longarm salvaged the sidesaddle and Cindy's possibles along with her hired harness, and rejoined her to toss them in the wagon bed atop his original load.

Then he helped her up into the snow-frosted seat, which they both had sense enough to brush off before sitting, and soon they were on their way. They had little warning as to how the winds were picking up until they crested the next rise and Longarm, at least, was chilled to the bone in no time.

The gal next to him must have felt some of it, despite his sheepskin mackinaw and the wool scarf wrapped over her pinned-up brown hair, for she asked him in a worried tone, "Aren't you *freezing* in that denim jacket, Custis?"

He allowed he was. But before he could explain he meant to get on down the lee side of this windy rise before he broke out a Hudson Bay four-pointer blanket from his own bedroll, she'd flung open the front of his mackinaw to say, "Well, no matter what Queen Victoria may or may not approve of, we can't have you freezing to death before we can get to some better shelter. Don't you suppose we could both fit inside a big old coat like this, if we, ah, sat sort of close?"

He knew better than to mention blankets at a time like this. They had to put their heads as well as their butts together before they'd worked it out. But in the end they wound up with his left arm down one sleeve so he could manage the team, with the other sleeve empty so he could hold Cindy tight against his side with both their heads stuck out the same woolly collar. It would have been comical as hell if anyone else had been looking.

She had one of her own arms around his waist as if to hold their already confined forms closer. He was glad he'd taken a shower that morning and put on duds fresh from the Chinese laundry around the corner. He could tell without asking that she'd started her day with fresh unmentionables and plenty of lilac water as well. Although by this time the two of them had been up and about long enough to start smelling a bit more natural, and it was a caution how inspired a man could be by the natural smells of a healthy woman. He wondered how much of his own smells might be getting through his clean cotton and bay rum.

He decided it was safer to ask how come she'd started out to ride forty miles in a late blizzard. She explained that they hadn't warned her it was fixing to snow while they were sticking her with a spavined mount. She was on her way to Kiowa because her married-up sister was feeling poorly and could use some help with her chores on what sounded to Longarm like a hardscrabble homestead. Cindy didn't know what her older sister and her brother-in-law were trying to raise on short-grass prairie west of Latitude 100. She didn't even know how close they were to proving their government claim, or what Longarm meant when he asked. So he asked her to tell him more about her own pretty self, a subject she seemed to know better.

Lucinda Ann Fuller made and sold dresses in Aurora, a stage stop east of Denver. Like himself, she'd taken time out to help somebody less fortunate, that overworked sister in her case. When she asked Longarm more about his own reasons for floundering on in an ever-growing blizzard, he wasn't sure she could hear every word of his reply. For the wind was really howling, and you could barely see five yards ahead of those snow-frosted mule ears now.

But she'd asked politely, so he said, "Jeff Wade rode herd with me when I first tried my hand at that not long after the

8

war. I had me a heap to learn, and made some mistakes that could have killed me if old Jeff hadn't been there to offer me a hand or a friendly word of warning, depending on what I was doing dumb."

She said his friend Jeff sounded nice.

Longarm said, "He was smarter too. He'd punched cows before the war, being a few years older than me and having left home sooner. As time passed by old Jeff married up, and I got too smart to tend other men's cows for forty-and-found as well. But we kept in casual touch over the years, with him and his family building their own herd out ahead, and me riding for Marshal Billy Vail and Uncle Sam back yonder in Denver. So a couple of days ago, I got this call for help from old Jeff. Jeff and a proddy neighbor seem to have worked themselves into one of them dumb standoffs calling for either a range war or a windmill."

There was no way to point, under their shared sheepskin, without her mistaking the motion for a sneaky feel-up. So he could only say, "That's mostly a windmill kit I'm hauling in back of us, along with some household supplies, play-pretties for Jeff's kids, and some lace curtains and ribbon bows for Miss Agatha, his woman. You see, they've been fenced off from a nearby year-round branchwater they'd been drawing on since they first filed three or four years back. I'm asking you to just take my word on some details of the Homestead Act of 1862. I ain't too sure about some of it my ownself, but in sum, Jeff was allowed to file on one quarter section or a hundred and sixty acres. No more. No less. He naturally drove his benchmarks around as dry and level a quarter section as he could, letting that nearby branchwater flow shallow or deep as it wanted across unclaimed open range."

She repressed a shiver and tried in vain to snuggle closer as she observed, "I think Sis did say they had a hundred and sixty acres, with eighty drilled for barley, forty left as meadow, and the rest growing winter silage and household truck out back."

Longarm shrugged without thinking. It felt swell. Then he told her, "I'm sure your brother-in-law thinks he knows what he's doing. Most of the smart boys out our way feel safer raising beef on short-grass in such an uncertain climate. We all know a cow needs five acres or more of marginal range to get by on. So you'd do well raising a dozen inside the official boundary lines of one homestead claim. But the loophole is the sort of contrariwise Open Range Acts of the same Land Management Office of the Department of the Interior."

Cindy said, "Sis wrote to me about that. They seemed to have lots of trouble with stockmen driving cows across their crops before Wes—that's my brother-in-law—strung plenty of barbed wire all around."

Longarm nodded. "That's how come they invented bobwire. Hedgerows take too long to grow, and any other sort of fencing can run dear by the time you've strung a mile of it."

She said, "I think Sis said their place is a quarter of a mile by a quarter of a mile. I see what you mean. Sis did say they'd lost a lot of seed money on that fencing, and that those stockmen had no right to be so mean to homesteaders."

Longarm smiled thinly. "Stockmen *are* homesteaders as often as not, out here on these High Plains. You have to claim *some* fool place as your base of operations, and when Abe Lincoln came up with his Homestead Act during the war, he made little or no distinction as to what he expected you to *raise* on your government claim, as long as you got all these Western territories populated enough to qualify for statehood and get him more senators who saw things his way. Back in old Abe's Illinois, a hundred and sixty acres for little more than the filing fee and five years of tending the land was a right handsome proposition. A quarter section is double the size of your average Eastern farm. But getting back to these

High Plains, your best bet is to claim and improve your own quarter section as your home spread, and then let your cows graze far and wide on open range nobody has seen fit to file on yet. Land Management would as soon have somebody using all that open country, if only to keep the buffalo and Mister Lo, the Poor Indian, on such public lands as the Great White Father figures they ought to need."

She shrugged, or shivered. "It sounds terribly complicated to me. What's supposed to happen once all that open range has been claimed and fenced in by other homesteaders, Custis?"

He said, "You just now heard me say the right hand of the Interior Department didn't seem to know what the left hand was doing, and did I mention the War Department? Miss Libby Custer is still in mourning for her soldier blue because the Bureau of Indian Affairs said one thing whilst the Bureau of Mines said another. But getting down to brass tacks closer to here and now, my pal Jeff Wade just met up with some of that trouble you and everyone but Land Management seems to have foreseen. I told you the Wades had been watering themselves and their fair-sized herd from a nearby branchwater running on down to Kiowa Creek, Jeff says. So now another cattle outfit, a bigger one, has fenced Jeff and his own needs off from the only all-year water for many a mile, and Jeff's first notion was to gather together some old pals, such as me, and have it out with the cruel and unusual neighbors six-gun and wire-cutter-style."

She gasped. "Brrr, and I'm not just talking about the wind I can't seem to keep out of my skirts down yonder. I've heard of the nasty little wars they've had between such factions. But what was that you said about a windmill, Custis?"

He said, "They just got over a nasty war indeed down New Mexico way, with the leaders on both sides wiped out, financially and physically, and nobody knowing where Billy the Kid may be hiding out at the moment. I wrote Jeff I'd scout him up the wherewithal for a tube well, a sunflower windmill kit, and such, to save everyone the financial and physical expenses of a blood feud with near neighbors. For as any Pawnee or Cheyenne could tell you, there's just no way to end a blood feud with near neighbors unless you kill every one down to the cradle babes of distant cousins. Someone is always going to grow up and come gunning in the years to follow unless you do."

She didn't seem to understand how you won a blood feud with any windmill kit. So he explained. "You don't have to win wars unless you declare 'em. Jeff's claim is high and dry betwixt the headwaters of the Box Elder and Kiowa Creeks, each in its own right a worthy rival of Denver's all-year Cherry Creek. He's still got plenty of open range for his cows to the west. It's that running water they can't get at now causing all the hard feelings. So like I wrote Jeff, it stands to reason the water table can't lay all that deep betwixt all-year creeks running no more than five or six miles apart. I read this geology book a spell back. It explained how these plains are just glorified mud pies carried down out of the Rockies by a few million years' worth of flash flooding. So we ought to be able to drive a tube well down through nothing but sand, silt, and clay to the same aquifer that feeds all these prairie streams that just spring up out here miles from the mountains. That's what you call beds of mighty wet sand and gravel, aquifers."

She said that did sound like safer work than gunfighting. Then, as the winds moved faster and faster, the team out ahead stopped dead in the fetlock-deep snow, and refused to budge forward no matter how Longarm whipped their stubborn mule asses with the slack of the reins.

He shrugged out of the loose mackinaw as he set the wheel brakes and handed her the reins. "I'd best go see what's balking them out here in the middle of nowheres."

The wind cut through his denims like a knife until, like a kid jumping into a mountain tarn on a hot day, he got more used to it and just let the wind sort of blow him along to where the two mules stood staring down at nothing much.

A man as stubborn might have cussed 'em out and whupped 'em good. Army mules had gained a reputation for willful contrariness, getting cussed and whupped by army recruits with even less common sense. Longarm had met army mules before. So he quietly told them, "I suspect some sneak laid a cattle guard yonder. Anyone can see the end of his drift fence to either side of the road. You boys just stay put and I'll have me a look-see, hear?"

Neither mule answered. Longarm hadn't expected them to. But his soothing words and reasonable attitude seemed to calm them some.

He strode on until one boot sank deeper than expected in the soft snow. He wagged his toe tip back and forth and, sure enough, felt the invisible timbers, railroad ties, or cottonwood logs someone else had lain across the dip they'd scooped between the fence posts to either side. He muttered something about public rights-of-way as he moved back to the wagon box and called up, "Drift fence with a cattle guard buried under the snow, but not deep enough for our team. I might be able to clear away the snow and ginger them across by hand afoot. But there's a quicker way. I'm telling you all this because I never wanted to scare you. I'm going back to lead the team off the road. It may be bumpy. But just sit tight a minute and I won't really turn this whole wagon upside down on you."

She had a better idea, she said. She got down to follow on foot as Longarm led the the team off the wagon trace with a short grip on the reins. They hadn't moved far when Cindy asked what seemed to be looming ahead in the tricky light and swirling snow.

13

He said, "Tumbleweeds, piled up along the fence by the winds as more form than substance. But they might be slowing the winds a tad, judging by the way the snow's piling up on the lee side."

He led the team a bit closer, and handed her the reins as he told her, "I doubt they'll want to turn into the wind, and you can see all that bobwire staring them in their fool faces. But hang on tight in any case. What I'm out to try involves drawing some staples so we can flatten the wire and drive on through without cutting it. I ain't sure anyone had a permit to string this drift fence here, but at least they had the decency to leave the public road open, even though these mules don't like cattle guards."

She took the reins, but stayed close as possible as Longarm got to work on the staples with his pocketknife. He had some fencing tools in one saddlebag, but right now he was in a hurry and his hands were turning blue and going numb on him. So he just yanked out the staples and let them land in the snow as they saw fit. Either there'd be enough tension left to hold the loose wire off the ground or there wouldn't. He was getting to where he just didn't give a shit.

He got enough slack to flatten the three strands of drift wire into the snow, got Cindy to stand on them, and led the team onward until the tailgate of the wagon box was through. Then he called out for her to rejoin him, and she did, his oversized mackinaw flapping around her in the wild winds until she too was in the lee of the mules and, better yet, that four-foot wall of tumbleweed and snowdrift. When she commented on how gently the snow seemed to fall on this side of that drift fence, Longarm said, "I noticed. I can't say as much for anywhere else out this way, and that sky up yonder is getting darker, not lighter, as this mighty grim day wears on. So if it's all the same with you, I vote we make day camp here and just wait for this fool blizzard to blow itself out."

She hesitated. "I don't know, Custis. I've heard of blizzards lasting as long as three days at a time out here on the High Plains."

"So have I," he said. "I've seen folks dug out of snowdrifts after spending a week or more on ice as well. Neither one of us started out this morning dressed like an Eskimo or packing snowshoes. Meanwhile, there may not be this much shelter within a dozen miles in any direction. So we'd best make use of what little we have."

She stared all about at the swirling snow. "I hope you know what you're talking about, Custis. If you call this shelter, I'd hate to be with you when you were roughing it!"

Chapter 2

It felt like at least a hundred Januaries. But it really took Longarm less than an hour to perform what Cindy described as the greatest wonder she'd ever witnessed.

The chest-high snowdrifts downwind of the fence line sloped the wrong way, of course. But Longarm soon fixed that with a poacher's shovel from the hired wagon's tool chest. He chose the dagger-bladed implement over their wider ash-scoop because the late-spring snow was heavier than it looked and he was out to move it with some care as to where it wound up.

He cut a vertical wall downwind, and patted the snow he dug atop it to where the blizzard was bouncing across that fence line a good five feet above the cleared sod. Then he ran the wagon broadside against the wall, shifted the wagon tarp partway off the load in the bed, and soon had a snow-covered canvas lean-to on that side.

He spread the bedroll off his saddle in what Cindy called a dear little cavern, under the wagon box and between the wheels. He'd have never finished without the sole custody of that one mackinaw. So he told Cindy to get into his bedding in just her riding habit while he did some more serious chores out there in the blamed blizzard.

It felt so good to shrug on that warm sheepskin mackinaw that he almost came in his jeans. Then he got to work with that shovel some more to cut a deeper, narrower niche in the snowbank for the mules. He knew they'd be warmer close together. So he packed the surplus snow to either side to form a sort of Eskimo stall. Then he broke out their feed bags and put a couple of fistfuls of cracked corn and snow in each before he stuck them on the worried brutes' muzzles. Then he unhitched them from the wagon tongue, and had no trouble leading them into the far less windy shelter. It was easy to tether them to the fence post he found handy to the windward wall of their niche. Then he told them he was sorry that was as much as he could do for them just now, and ran back to duck under the wagon box with Cindy.

He told her, "I know we've just met, Miss Cindy. But I'm still going to have to get inside that bedroll with you, unless you expect a side of frozen beef to dig us out once it lets up."

She demurely replied, "Don't be silly. We're both fully dressed and to tell the truth, it's not so warm in here alone."

So he shucked the mackinaw, wadded it up to form a pillow for the two of them, and removed his gun rig and snow-crusted boots as well, before sliding in beside her. He'd put that roll together with just his own husky frame in mind. So fully dressed or not, the two of them fit sort of snug. But as Cindy herself observed when Longarm apologized, the whole fool notion was designed to keep the two of them warm, and they'd never have to tell Queen Victoria or anyone else how they might have kept from freezing to death in an April Fool blizzard.

Longarm planted his rolled-up gun rig in his overturned Stetson with the grips handy and said, "I got some canned beans and tomato preserves in yon saddlebags, betwixt the front wheels. But it may take this storm a while to blow over. So if you don't mind a late supper . . ."

She said, "Heavens, it can't be much past noon, despite that dark sky up yonder. How long do you imagine we'll be snowed in here?"

Longarm could *imagine* being snowed in for days. It hadn't been so bad that time he'd been stuck in that mountain cabin with those two frisky gals who'd wanted to be warmed up bare-ass.

He told himself not to think about three naked bodies between the blankets when he was rubbing hips with a dressmaking gal in full skirts who kept talking about Queen Victoria. To change the subject he said, "I wish I'd rolled this bedding for winter travel. We could sure use a couple of extra blankets."

She blinked in surprise and replied, "Could we? I was just about to say I'm almost *too* warm in here. Would you be shocked if a lady unfastened just two teeny buttons of this bodice?"

He chuckled and said, "Not hardly. I wasn't talking about the two of *us* needing more blankets. But them mules are still partly exposed to that threatening sky you just mentioned, and as the snow fluttering straight down lands on their bare hides, it's sure to melt, and should it get any colder . . ."

"Oh, the poor things!" she said. "What if we covered them with *my* bedding, Custis?"

He frowned thoughtfully and replied, "I don't recall no bedroll on that sidesaddle of your'n, Miss Cindy."

She explained, "I hired the saddle in Aurora along with that sick horse. But I naturally packed my personal saddlebags before I ever went to that livery stable. I wasn't planning on camping out like this. So the summer-weight bedding I meant to use at my sister's place is in one of my bags, along with my nightgown and, ah, some unmentionables."

18

Longarm propped himself up on one elbow. "You won't want to use nothing that's been aboard a wet mule before it's been washed good with naphtha soap, Miss Cindy. But seeing you're being such a sport, and seeing we've still got a ways to go behind them mules, I'd be a fool not to take you up on your kind offer."

So she told him the bedding was in the near or left-side saddlebag as he crawled back out, surprised at how grim that felt after a short warm spell in his bedroll. He moved over to the saddles on his hands and knees and broke out the two flannel blankets she'd said he'd find near the top. He found her nightgown to be made of real silk. He tried not to consider what her small warm body might feel like sincerely dressed for bed. He found something else she'd already called unmentionable. That was something to study on as well. Victorian ladies had all sorts of unmentionable notions, from corset covers to India-rubber douche bags, that they never talked about in front of menfolk. So it was possible old Cindy figured no mere man would understand just what that small oilcloth-covered kit was designed to prevent.

Possible, but hardly likely. How many gals that cautious about their sex lives could take a full-grown man with a mustache for a virgin child? And she'd held out on those extra blankets, as he'd held out on his, when she'd suggested they share that one mackinaw!

First things coming first, Longarm hauled the bedding out to the mules, the flannel flapping in the wind once he rose to his full height, and used their harness to secure the pink and mauve blankets in place tucked under the horse collars at one end so their big brown rumps were still half exposed at the other. Cindy didn't want mule shit on her bedding in any case.

He knew any cover was better than none. He was feeling the cold through his own damp denim by the time he'd rejoined

Cindy under warm dry bedding. She said, "Good heavens! You're sopping wet! Why don't you slip out of your jacket and jeans at least? I mean, it's not as if anyone could *see* anything, right?"

He knew he was supposed to say something more modest. But in point of fact he just told her it was a grand notion, and soon had himself down to his cotton undershirt and long underwear. It felt far warmer as soon as he had his damp outerwear spread to dry, or at least try to, on the damp grass under the wagon box.

Then he asked, seeing she was such a sport about formalities, if he had her permission to smoke, and when she said he did, whether she'd care to share a three-for-a-nickel cheroot with him.

She giggled, and allowed he was teaching her all sorts of bad habits that afternoon as he lit up. Then she confessed that, like a lot of ladies, she did indulge privately in the vices of nicotine. He hoped she meant she smoked on the sly. He hated to kiss gals who'd been chewing or dipping snuff.

She hadn't said she wanted him kissing her. So he didn't for a spell. They jawed about this and that, mostly about the storm, as they passed the lit cheroot back and forth. He answered those few questions she asked about his own past. He was pleased to see she volunteered hardly any details about her own. He'd found women of the world who packed sanitary supplies along had two ways of talking to a man they were bedded down with. The smarter ones didn't talk all that much about when they'd first noticed boys and girls were built different. The other kind seemed to feel a man really cared to hear about all the other men who'd used, abused, and betrayed them in the all too recent past.

They smoked two cheroots down before Longarm fumbled his pocket watch out of his nearby rumpled jacket and declared, "Oh, Lord, I thought it was surely later than that.

The kids are still in school this afternoon back in town. But do you reckon you could hold out past nightfall before we have a light and late supper?"

She sighed. "I agree it makes sense to husband our trail supplies until we know how long they may have to last. To tell the truth, I'm not half as hungry as *bored*! I don't mean I find your droll conversation boring, Custis. It's just that I'm not used to being in bed at this time of day, with nothing to do but just laze about like a slugabed in some old Turk's harem!"

He chuckled and said, "I've often wondered what they do all day in those harems as well. For all we really know, those harem gals do close-order drill or mend socks. It ain't as if any Christian but that English writer Richard Burton ever got in and out of a harem in one piece, and I ain't sure I buy his yarns about them. I didn't know gals speculated about harem life as well. I've always figured them Turkish notions were designed so the menfolk would have the most fun, just as Queen Victoria's current rules are set up to favor you ladies."

She pouted. "The devil you say! Where did you ever get the wild idea that the Widow of Windsor's fusty social code was meant to be fun for *anyone?*"

He shrugged a bare shoulder. "Somebody must be getting something out of forbidding musicians to describe what holds a piano off the floor in vulgar anatomical terms. As a lawman I get to enforce some mighty odd laws from time to time, and I often suspect that next to sinning, there's nothing like forbidding others to sin when it comes to having fun!"

She laughed. "I've noticed that. I absolutely forbid you to kiss me, even though we are snowed in alone miles from any old fuss who could possibly scold us."

He got rid of their smoke before he hauled her in to kiss her as if they were old pals. From the way she kissed back,

21

he knew a man would have been a fool to try and manage that much hot stuff at once. It was her idea to grab for his privates through the fly of his long underwear before he'd worked his free hand any lower than her firm left tit. But since she was stroking him so friendly, it felt natural to just hoist her voluminous serge skirts. Then seeing she'd been riding with nothing under them, he simply rolled into the soft bared love saddle between her welcoming thighs.

But even as he took his old organ-grinder back from her to guide it on to paradise with his own hand, she gasped, "Oh, dear, this is so sudden! Don't you think we ought to take all our clothes off first?"

To which he replied, parting her love-lips with his hot turgid head, "What's the hurry? We got a whole day and likely a whole night to try it every which way. Right now I'm fixing to waste my wad way in the middle of the air!"

So she hugged him closer, crooning that waste was a crime, and then, as he thrust it deeper, she gasped, "Oh, Lordy! Is all that meant for little old me?" Then, try as he might, he just couldn't hold back in such pleasant surroundings.

He could tell she'd been wanting it for quite a spell too. She responded in kind with the skillful hip movements of a gal who'd doubtless done a lot of riding, and vice versa. He was glad she liked to kiss French and screw the way most country folks liked to eat, with little or no conversation as they simply satisfied their natural healthy appetites.

He came ahead of her. Any man would have. But she felt so fine on his shaft he was able to keep going after a couple of gulping gasps. So he had her coming herself a short while later, and she allowed he'd been right about her wanting him to screw her silly since she'd first rubbed hips with him and smelled his clean manly crotch in the warmth of that heavy mackinaw.

He had her stripped down to no more than her black lisle stockings, and they were going at it sidesaddle with him naked as a jay when Cindy suddenly gasped, "Good heavens! I think the sun just came out again, Custis!"

He had to twist some to follow her gaze out across the sunlit blinding snow. Once he had, he laughed, thrust into her again, and said, "When you're right you're right. I told you it had to blow over sooner or later, But this one was a real April Fool joke, and I sure feel foolish!"

She purred, "I can take a joke, but you're starting to feel sort of soft as well. Do we have time to work it up some more before we have to push on, darling?"

He started moving it in and out of her some more as he replied, "This day's fair shot. So we could show up at old Jeff's after he and his own woman have likely gone to bed with much the same notions in mind. Or we could just stay here right comfortable, and shoot for an early start and a noon arrival tomorrow. It's up to you, Miss Cindy. Are you really anxious about getting to your sister's place?"

To which the passionate dressmaker demurely replied, "She's made out up to now without my help, and I haven't made love so swell in a coon's age. So I vote we stay put. And could I get on top, now that it's getting warm enough to throw off the top bedding?"

Chapter 3

Whoever first said virtue was its own reward had never spent much time on the High Plains in April. For they were really glad they'd camped overnight with a night fire burning just outside their wagon-box love-nest, and were able to get an early start after a lot of lazing to go with all that loving, smoking, and cold canned grub. The day dawned shirtsleeve-warm after a still starry night, and to say the going was slow was to compliment the condition of the old post road.

A lot of snow had evaporated directly into the thin dry air above the High Plains. But enough of it melted the old-fashioned way to gumbo the wagon ruts considerably as they wound across what now resembled the horizon-to-horizon hide of a pinto alligator. The green blotches were growing as the white patches turned to slush under a cloudless bowl of cobalt blue, with a big raw sun glaring down as if in disbelief at the remains of that unseasonable snowstorm. Longarm had already explained it had to snow like hell for better than a full day to qualify as an official blizzard. She allowed it had still been a lot of fun.

The steady old mules, relieved of Cindy's blankets, hauled the heavily laden wagon better than horses the same size might have, with the sticky mud clinging to their hooves and caked to the wheel rims as if Longarm was out to invent some new fat brand of rubberized tire. Some of the draws were fetlock to stirrup-deep in ice-cold meltwater. That was rough on the stock, but served to lighten the mud-caked wheels and underchassis from time to time as they splashed on to the southeast, slower or faster as the post road ran upgrade or downgrade.

They lost more time more than once when they came upon drift fences Longarm didn't recall from his last ride out this way the summer before last. He was sure most of the empty-looking country all about was still open range. Drift fences were a recent notion, whether state laws permitted them or not. A drift fence wasn't meant to pen anything in or out. Thanks to how cheap bobwire seemed to keep getting, stockmen could afford to erect a few miles of what seemed a pointless enter-prise on any survey map. You drove your first post and kept driving more till you'd left three or more strands of discour-agement that would steer, or drift, free-ranging cows away from where you didn't want to look for them or toward where you'd find them easier to manage. Cindy said she understood why stockmen wouldn't want their beef holed up in a timbered draw at roundup time, grazing along a railroad track, or just wandering too far across a rolling sea of grass. She had more trouble grasping the way cattle guards worked.

It would have been unlawful to run a drift fence smack across a federal post road, and swing gates could be a bother to all concerned. But thanks to the way cows and most hooved critters viewed their world as they grazed it, you could keep them from strolling through a gap in a fence by laying a shallow depression there, with cross-timbers set close enough for wheels to roll across with no more than a tingle. Even a kid could walk through a cattle guard whether he stepped from cross-timber to cross-timber or down in the slots between them. Most human beings found it easier to step on the timbers. Dogs and ponies, if you got down and led them, seemed better able to manage by stepping in the cracks. But no cow with any choice in the matter seemed to want to even think about the grass on the other side of a cattle guard. That was why there were so many guards over this way, despite the fact that no cows were around.

When Cindy had asked about that, Longarm explained that the April Fool's joke had likely driven a lot of stock down out of sight into the draws all around. She already knew there was less wind once you got down off the rises. As they drove along he swept his free hand in a wide horizontal arc, explaining, "What looks like miles and miles of empty prairie all about is really just the tops of the rises. It was George Armstrong Custer who warned in an army manual on Indian fighting that you could hide whole Indian villages just off the beaten path in a fairly shallow draw."

He wrinkled his nose and added, "He was right. Nobody who read his instructions has ever been able to fathom how old George managed to ride that close to so many Indians without suspecting any worth mention were there. Terry had sent him out *looking* for Indians, and old George had written the book on *finding* them."

He pointed off to their right and said, "Yonder's a cow. Looks to be a Cherokee, black Scotch breed mixed with Texas longhorn. Good breed for this sort of range."

She stared blankly. "I don't see any cow over that way, darling. Are you sure you're not just teasing me again, the way you did me last night about you and that French actress?"

He said, "I wasn't teasing you about Miss Sarah Bernhardt when I said I didn't know whether she did it that way or not. I was sent to bodyguard her on her first American tour, not to mess with her body. As to that cow you seem to suspect I just made up, it's right there in plain sight. Just a bit to the west of that smoke plume on the horizon."

Cindy stared hard. "Smoke plume? Oh, now I see it, I think. You must have eyes like a hawk with glasses. Land's sake! That *does* look like a black cow over that way, unless it's a horsefly on the far side of Main Street back in Aurora!"

He said it was more likely a Cherokee beef critter. "I see another one now. Pure Texas calico with chongo horns. And yep, there rises a fawn calf, likely part Jersey. Somebody's ranging a herd of catch-as-catch-can scrub out this way. We'll see more as they come out of the draws to graze. They got these Hindu cows down Mexico way who like to play in mud puddles. But most cows with any resemblance to longhorns are descended from wild North African cows that would rather chew cuds of sun-cured grass with a pinch of dust in it."

Cindy asked, "Who do you suppose that smoke goes with, darling?"

Longarm shrugged. "Too far off to worry about. From the way it's rising, they must be out to dry a damp soddy good after all that unusual weather. Ain't nobody on fire, though. Wrong color for woodsmoke. Looks like they've stuffed a heap of damp cow chips in a heating stove with not enough draft. Probably new nesters homesteading out this way without a heap of experience or even common sense. Takes the average nester gal no more than a few smoky tries to learn you ought to let a cow chip dry out all the way before you toss it in your stove."

Cindy said, "It can't be my sister then. That smoke's rising in about the right direction, but my sister and brother-in-law have burned many a cow chip by now. I've burned some myself. I don't know about damp ones. I know they burn clean and nearly smokeless after a summer baking in the sun."

Longarm chuckled. "When old Jeff Wade and me herded beef together down around Dodge, nesters along the trail would come out offering to coffee and cake the whole outfit free if we'd like to run the herd into a handy fenced forty and set a spell. We were as willing, if the offer came near a natural time for a trail break. We knew they were offering because a fair-sized herd could deposit one whole lot of cook-stove fuel in no more than an hour or so. But we were getting free coffee and cake out of the deal, so it evened out fair to both sides."

Cindy laughed, gasped, and suddenly blurted out, "My Lordy, less than twenty-four hours ago I was calling you good sir, and now here we are jawing about cow shit, as if it was the most natural subject."

He clucked the mules up the next rise as he calmly assured her that cow shit was perfectly natural and that nothing they'd said or done since they'd met seemed unnatural to him.

She replied pensively, "I know how you feel about nature. I still think you did it with that infamous if divine Sarah Bernhardt, who was noted for her natural feelings as well."

He was saved from having to defend the reputation of a nice old gal who'd only kissed him once, in a sisterly fashion, after he'd saved her life out Virginia City way. Suddenly Claire gasped in dismay as they topped the rise to send a black puff of carrion crows skyward from the dead dogie they'd been pecking at in the slushy bottom of the draw beyond.

Knowing how mules felt about the smell of death, Longarm reined them off the wagon trace to windward so they could haul the wagon well clear of the downed critter and across clean wet grass. But Cindy could see well enough to declare, "Oh, dear, somebody shot the poor thing in the eye!"

Longarm shook his head slightly. "The crows did that. They always start with the eyeballs, unless Mister Lo has opened a body wider for 'em with his scalping knife. I'd say this reads more like a stray dogie getting spooked by that wicked wind, blinded by all that snow, and drowning itself over yonder while bawling for its mama."

She objected, "There's not that much meltwater down here, dear."

He said, "Not now there ain't. But look how the grass has all been combed the same way up the slopes to either side. There's just no saying which particular draw is apt to flood higher than the others all about. But as a rule of thumb, it's best not to be down in any draw on the rare occasions it rains or snows on this range. Lots of outfits will have lost stock to that April Fool's joke we just got through on higher ground, honey. Sudden floods after the fall roundup don't catch as many childish cows. It's the ones around this time of the year that cost you the most beef, or make that veal, since most critters have learned to take better care of themselves by the time they're beef."

They came upon another dead dogie a few furlongs on. This one's demise was tougher to fathom, until Longarm considered all the snow that wasn't there anymore and the way the critter's head hung a good six inches clear of the grass through another bobwire fence. He told Cindy, "Blizzard chased it along this rise until it hit that drift fence. It got hung up instead of drifting off to the east the way it was meant to. Then the snow piled up around it high enough to freeze it to death. It would have been better off halfway down the far slope. But that's the trouble with brand-new beef. It ain't got much sense. You either find it high on a windswept rise or down in the very bottom of a flooded draw after the weather clears. Either way, there's little you can do but salvage the hide before the carrion critters rip it useless."

He reined in for the cattle guard to the right of the dead dogie as he added, "Sometimes a haunch of beef is worth salvaging, when you know for sure how a critter died and it ain't been dead too long."

He got down to lead the mules through the cattle guard, muttering curses about people who'd been stringing so much wire on open range across public rights-of-way.

They drove on less than an hour before, atop another rise, Longarm pointed ahead. "The Wades' spread lies beyond that rise with all the soap-weed growing along the crest. I remember that bodacious growth from the last time I was over this way. Like I promised, we'll be there early enough to invite to noon dinner."

Then, as they drove closer, Longarm thoughtfully added, "I don't recall no fence line along that rise, though. Somebody around these parts must be a thundering wonder at selling bobwire."

Driving on, he added, "I once played cards with old Bet-A-Million Gates, the bobwire salesman. He let me win, and took it like a sport when he found out I wasn't in the market for the famous brand he sells by the day's ride. But I've often suspected he gets a heap of prospects too drunk and jolly to know what they're fencing. Them four strands up ahead are an example of what I mean. Three strands are more than you need to drift cows. You use four to stop 'em cold."

Cindy said she thought her brother-in-law had fenced their homestead with four expensive strands of Glidden wire.

Longarm nodded. "That's what I meant. That can't be any fenced claim line up ahead. It only makes sense, sort of, as a way to keep free-ranging stock out of the draw beyond. Only I remember range I've been over more than once, and there ain't nothing to worry a cow in the shallow open draw beyond them soap-weeds."

Then he scowled and declared, "Now that's just silly!" as he saw that the solidly strung fence ran smack across the post road with neither a gate nor a cattle guard.

Cindy said, "I don't see any housing around here, darling. But why couldn't that be a claim line? It seems to run due east and west, the way most homestead claims are laid out."

Longarm shook his head. "You just heard me say that can't be a claim line, and I never make flat statements unless they make sense. Land Management could never record a homestead claim smack across a federal post road if it wanted to. The Postmaster General would never stand for it."

Cindy suggested, "Maybe this particular federal road has been abandoned. Didn't the government abandon that freight and postal route up to the Montana gold fields a few years ago, dear?"

Longarm reined in and set the wheel brakes as he made a wry face and said, "The Bozeman Trail was never abandoned to homesteaders. A Lakota general called Mahpiua Luta shut it down on us after winning what everyone but the army calls Red Cloud's War."

He moved around to the tool chest strung along the near side of the wagon box. "The Bozeman's open to us Wasichu again these days. The government scrapped the Sioux Treaty of '68 after they buried Custer and his boys in '76. Some Indians I know hold that was mighty unfair of us. But I ain't sure anyone could expect a peace treaty to hold water after they went and wiped out a third of the Seventh Cavalry."

He found the long-handled wire cutters he was looking for. Then he ambled ahead to the fence, continuing in a conversational tone she had to strain to make out. "You can't expect others to respect your own feelings unless you consider those of others. I don't see any Christian reason for stringing four strands of bob across this federal right-of-way. So I'm going to just clear this post road for the Postmaster General in my federal capacity and considerable annoyance."

He did. It only took a few moments to cut the four strands, close to the fence posts on either side of the wagon trace, and neatly drape the severed lengths clear of the wagon ruts but off the sod and easy enough to find, should somebody have a more reasonable use for, say, a hundred feet of bob.

He put the cutters away, shut the tool chest, and climbed back up beside Cindy to drive on. When she asked if what he'd done wasn't likely to vex someone considerably, Longarm shrugged and told her he was sort of vexed himself.

He explained patiently. "No private citizen has any right to fence off a public thoroughfare. How would the two of us ever get to the Wade spread, or your sister's beyond, if any fool with a roll of bob was allowed to string fences that blocked our constitutional rights to get there?"

She allowed his words made sense. Then she commenced to pin up her brown hair, lest the ladies ahead suspect she'd been rolling about on the ground with some masterful lawman.

It only took a few minutes to drive another half mile. So she was just pinning her small brown derby in place atop her tresses when Longarm reined in again, exclaiming, "Aw, come on, this joke has gone just about far enough!"

He was already climbing back down as Cindy saw what the trouble was and exclaimed, "Another fence across the road out here in the middle of nowhere?"

Longarm was too pissed to answer as he broke out the wire cutters again and stormed forward afoot. But he was naturally enough of a thinker to gaze all about for some sign of a homestead in what sure seemed a fenced-in homestead claim. That is, if homesteaders had been allowed to file smack across a federal road.

He made the same short work of the second fence line. But then he put the cutters away, hauled out his Winchester '73, and told Cindy to stay put as he had a little look-see along the mysterious fence line.

She called after him to be careful as he strode off to the west inside the fencing, levering a thoughtful round in the chamber of his saddle gun as he did so. Since a half mile was an easy walk even for a city lady, and since the fool rectangle was sliced catty-corner across its middle, Longarm

32

only had to stride a few rods before he could see that, sure enough, some pest had indeed strung four strands of bob around what would have been a quarter-section claim had one been remotely lawful there. It got even sillier when, try as he might, Longarm failed to find so much as a stack of lumber or pile of cut sods to indicate the intent of improving the claim, as the Homestead Act required.

Shaking his head, Longarm returned to the wagon, climbed back up beside Cindy, and leaned the Winchester against the dashboard their feet were braced against as he told her, "Like I said, somebody sure sells lots of bobwire to drunks around here. Mayhaps old Jeff up ahead can tell us who's gone loco so expensively."

She stared at him wide-eyed. "Crazy people frighten me, darling. When Sis and me were little, there was this old crazy lady who lived down the road. Everyone said she was harmless. But we were afraid of her and never went by her place after dark."

Longarm nodded, and said there seemed to be such an unfortunate old crone in most every neck of the woods.

Cindy shook her head. "Not as crazy as this one. Sis and me never got over how smart we'd been to avoid Miz Whittle, after the night she tore out her front gate after dark to chop both the Baxter twins dead with her meat cleaver!"

Longarm whistled softly and declared, "Let's hope there's nobody loco as that in these parts."

When she asked what he'd do if there was, he said soothingly, "Don't fret your pretty self, honey. I'm packing five in the wheel of my six-gun, two in my double derringer, and fifteen in this Winchester. So nobody is about to get near you with any meat cleaver, hear?"

She repressed a shudder. "What if we don't see one coming in time? Everyone said the Baxter twins could have outrun Miz Whittle easy, had not she caught them by surprise in the soft light of gloaming, with other kids playing kick-the-can just down the same road. Sometimes crazy people don't tell you what they mean to do to you, or even that they're after you. And didn't you say you were on your way to help old friends deal with some crazy neighbors?"

Longarm started to say Jeff Wade had written about trouble with an ornery neighbor, rather than a crazy one. But he held the thought as they drove on. For the drilling gear and windmill kit in the wagon bed was meant to calm a fuss about water with a run-of-the-mill range hog.

All bets were off if the rascal was *loco en la cabeza*!

Chapter 4

They made it to the Wade spread before high noon, just as Longarm had predicted, and Cindy was naturally greeted as if she'd been an old pal as well. Longarm didn't have many old pals who weren't naturally friendly.

Jeff Wade was a few inches shorter and eight or ten years older than Longarm, but didn't look like a man you'd want to mess with for no good reason. His woman, Miss Agatha, had filled out to be far more motherly than she'd looked waiting tables in Dodge a spell back. The two kids they had, six-year-old Judy and four-year-old Sonny, doubtless accounted for their mother's weary good looks. They took to calling Lucinda Fuller "Aunt Cindy" right off, and demanded she come around to the back of their soddy to admire the litter a mouser called Snuff had just given birth to under the hen house. They paid no mind when their mother told them to leave the lady be. But when old Jeff snapped his fingers once, they allowed Aunt Cindy could look at Snuff's kittens later.

Jeff had two hired hands, a Mexican and a younger Arapaho breed. So he told Longarm and Cindy to come right on in and let his help take care of the mule team while Miss Agatha dished out some grub.

To her credit, Cindy offered to help. But Agatha told her to just take a load off her feet at the table with the menfolk while young Judy learned a thing or two about kitchen chores.

Being a country boy in his own right, Longarm knew serious talk was supposed to wait until dessert and an after-dinner light-up while the ladies cleared the table. But as she sat down between Longarm and Jeff on the open veranda of the soddy, the April sun having gotten back to its more usual self, Cindy brought up the reason Jeff had sent for Longarm, and asked where they were getting water these days.

Jeff didn't get sore. Cindy was pretty, and even country rules were made to be broken. But he didn't sound too cheerful as he told them both, "Diego and Skinny haul it in our tank wagon from a couple of miles downstream. The long haul bubbles some of the stagnant taste out, and of course we boil it good after it's had the chance to settle clear."

He turned to Longarm. "That Duke Albright I writ you about hasn't fenced any further down the branchwater yet."

Cindy, trying to make sense of it, asked, "Is anyone allowed to do that? I thought a quarter section or a half mile each way was all you were allowed to claim and fence at one time."

Before Longarm could catch her eye Jeff morosely told her, "Duke Albright don't seem to know that, ma'am. When I had my lawyer call him on it in the county court, *his* lawyer said most of the bobwire cutting us off from water was drift fence. Albright's had two of his in-laws file proper on quarter sections up- and downstream from us. Like you just said, that only gave them the right to run a mile along what used to be our side of the branchwater between 'em. My lawyer is still fussing with their lawyers, plural, about what they claim they meant as a drift fence to keep their free-ranging stock on their side of the draw they share. They call Albright a duke because he's got the money to buy the backing it takes to behave like that. My lawyer, a nice kid, if you like kids, says fighting Duke Albright in court is like wrestling with one of them octaroon fish. But you know what they say the Sandwich Island pearl-divers do when they're attacked by an octaroon fish."

Longarm cut in to observe mildy, "I think you must mean octopus, Jeff. Folks out California way call C.S. Huntington of the Southern Pacific Railroad The Octopus for much the same reasons. Fighting a way richer cuss in court can be a bother, what with all the stays, postponings, and appeals he can afford to wrap around you."

Jeff Wade grumbled, "I just said that. Them pearl-divers waste no time on all them slithery arms an octaroon fish has. They bite his ugly head, right betwixt the eyes. That's where an octaroon fish has his brain, in this bitty peanut right betwixt his bigger eyes. So if you was to back my play as I just stood up to Duke Albright man to man, Custis . . ."

"Did I forget to mention I've been a lawman for some time now?" Longarm said, adding in a more soothing tone, "I wrote you I knew where I could get a good buy on a windmill kit and enough tubing to drive down into your water table."

"I wrote you right back that I didn't want you to go to that much trouble," Jeff said. "Me and mine can't afford the expense, and even if we could, Duke Albright has no right to fence us off from water we was using first!"

Longarm said, "I told you I got a good buy and it's my treat. I never did pay you back for that time you saved me from that midnight stampede, old pard."

Jeff was about to fuss at him, but Longarm turned to Cindy with a smile and explained, "We were moving eighteen hundred head across a bad stretch of the Staked Plains when lightning stampeded 'em in next-to-total darkness. I was riding a paint called Fandango, out front and trying to mill them, when she put a hoof wrong in the dark and spilled us both near the bottom of a rise in front of all that fast-moving beef."

Agatha had come in with her tray in time to catch her man griping about Longarm not owing him for anything. So she told Longarm to behave himself too. Then Longarm went on to Cindy. "I don't know how old Jeff here spotted me afoot in that light. But he did, and grabbed me on the fly as he cut across a sea wave of oncoming horns in the nick of time. So don't you think it's mean of him to say my living hide ain't worth at least as much as a modest load of hardware?"

Agatha set down her tray and turned to take a platter of soda biscuits from little Judy as she tried to back her man about Longarm not being beholden to anyone. But her heart wasn't in it once Longarm soberly asked, "Do you both figure killing a man or more has paying for a tube well beat once the roll is called up yonder?"

Jeff said, "Hold on. Nobody said nothing about killing nobody."

But Longarm insisted, "Yes, you did, Jeff. You said you wanted me to back you when you went up against this Duke Albright personal. Were you figuring on letting *him* kill *you*? Unless that's your divine plan, I fail to see how you're going to settle things that way without *somebody* dying."

As his woman dished out the sliced ham, baked beans, and fried potatoes, Jeff said, "I doubt Duke Albright has the hair on his chest for a man-to-man showdown. I figured if he was to see I'd had enough of his foolish tricks, and wasn't afraid of him . . ."

"Is *he* supposed to be afraid of *you*?" Longarm asked wearily as he nodded his thanks to little Judy, who was pouring a cup of coffee for him.

Turning back to her father, Longarm said, "I wish I had a nickel for every war that's been started by one gent expecting the other to crawfish back in fear instead of taking him up on his kind offer. I'm sure Abe Lincoln was supposed to run and hide under the bed as soon as those Carolina militiamen without an arms industry fired on Fort Sumter back in '61, speaking of April Fool jokes, but we all know how *that* turned out. So why don't we just sink you a tube well, throw up a windmill, and leave you all swimming in even sweeter water than you've ever hauled from that blamed draw?"

Agatha sat down to be coffeed by her tiny daughter as she allowed their old friend's words made sense. Then she had to send Judy back to the kitchen to serve her baby brother and the two hired hands, giving Jeff the chance to complain. "I'd be willing to water us and our stock from a hole in the ground, if that was all there was to Duke Albright's mischief. But he'd never leave us be. Skinny just told me yesterday about another fool fence line he spotted a few miles to the northwest up that post road. Skinny says they've strung the wire clean across the road. Which may be why you never got my answer to your dumb suggestions for a peaceable settlement, Custis."

Cindy said, "Ooh, I think I know the fencing you mean. Custis just cut it this morning!"

Longarm would have kicked her under the table. But the cat was out of the bag. So he just nodded and said, "Dumb place to string wire."

Jeff Wade stared soberly across the table at him. "You cut a man's fence, without his *permit*, Custis?"

To which Longarm could only reply, "Had to. Like I said, it was blocking the federal post road, and I'm a federal lawman."

He tried some of the potatoes—they were done just right— as Jeff said, "I'm sorry about the uncharitable opinion I was just entertaining about an old pal's grit, Custis. Once you've cut a man's fence, you don't have to go looking for him. He's supposed to come looking for *you* if he's any sort of man at all."

Longarm rinsed down the mouthful with coffee and said, "Aw, mush, Miss Cindy and me weren't declaring war on nobody. We were exercising our rights as free citizens to travel along a public thoroughfare. I didn't see anybody watching as I did what had to be done. There ain't a soul inhabiting that homestead claim, if that's what it's supposed to be."

Jeff said, "They're going to know *somebody* cut it. I hope you weren't meaning to light out and leave me and mine to explain when, not if, Duke Albright and his own hands come looking for some answers."

Longarm put down his knife and fork to stare severely at his host as he softly replied. "You're right. You've been entertaining some mighty uncharitable opinions. But I don't want to invite you to fight in front of your family, Jeff. So first we're going to see that Miss Cindy here gets safely on to her own kin's spread. Then we're going to sink that tube well, and if this Duke Albright ain't figured out who cut his dumb fencing, by then I aim to go tell him."

Jeff chortled, "Hot damn! Sorry, ladies. I can get a few of our friendlier neighbors to ride over with you, me, and my two-man crew!"

Longarm would have had to really tell the ladies he was sorry if he'd said what he wanted to out loud. Instead he said, "That ain't the civilized or even sensible way, Jeff. I mean to pin my badge to the front of this jacket and call on the wire-stringing cuss in my official capacity. I'm sure he has some explanation for barring passage along a federal post road. His lawyers couldn't have told him he had any right to. Whether I have to go fussing through homestead claims, riparian rights, and so on will depend a heap on how polite he answers. I'm expecting him to answer polite. Most men do, given the choice of that or a showdown with the federal government. I don't mean to low-rate you and your smallholder neighbors, Jeff, but it don't take as much grit to bully kids *your* size as it might to meet Uncle Sam after school."

40

Jeff Wade seemed to feel low-rated anyway. It took both gals and an extra helping of raisin pie to sooth his ruffled pride enough to go along with Longarm's plans, and he still said Longarm simply didn't grasp what an unreasonable bully Duke Albright could be.

Longarm said, "Bullies old enough to shave and retain a bunch of lawyers must have motives more grown-up than your average schoolyard bully, Jeff."

"Name me one then," Jeff challenged. "We've all of us studied on why Duke Albright's such an untidy neighbor, Custis. I thought first off he was out to force us smaller stockmen to sell out to him cheap. But my own kid lawyer pointed out, and I have to agree, it makes no sense to offer anything for unproven claims when more than ninety percent of the range all about is still public land for the asking!"

Longarm washed down some pie as he considered that. Then he had to nod. "Your lawyer's more than right. Nobody holding any homestead claim for less than five years could sell it at any price to anybody. You can leave an unproven claim to a lawful sole heir, so's he or she can go on occupying and improving the land the full five years the land office requires. But even if you elder Wades got hit by lightning, there'd be no way anyone could buy this claim off them kids in the kitchen for . . . How long does this homestead claim have to run, Jeff?"

Before her husband could answer Agatha Wade gasped, "Oh, my land, what would become of my Judy and Sonny if something happened to Jeff and me? Who would protect them from that awful Duke Albright and his army of toughs?"

Longarm said in a soothing tone, "Me, Miss Agatha. After that, as wards of the state, they'd have someone even more versed in the law appointed by a federal court to adminster this here estate that's still federal land, at least until the land office surrenders it fee-simple to the claim-holders and the tax rolls of Colorado. So all in all, a land thief would have a tougher row to hoe with this claim held by your orphans than if he tried to take it from you directly."

He turned back to Jeff and repeated his question about how long a time they were talking about.

Jeff said, "Eighteen months, the more fool I. Me and Aggie filed on an earlier claim further out on the plains, as you may recall."

When Longarm nodded Jeff explained. "The water was bad and there was too much jimson and not enough grass. So we abandoned that claim and filed on this better land about three and a half years back."

He stared soberly down at his empty pie plate. "I thought I knew what we were doing. The range all around is just fine, and we had plenty of all-year sweet-water until recent. Somebody should have drygulched that infernal Duke Albright when he horned in three years or less back."

Agatha rose to start clearing the table. Cindy got up to help her as the two men lit their smokes. Longarm got his cheroot going before he asked with a puzzled frown, "Are you saying this Albright cuss has barely settled in and he's already started picking fights with you?"

Jeff said, "Me and just about everyone else he can get at. I keep telling you that man's a dedicated bastard. But you seem to have wax in your ears."

He took a drag on his cigar and glanced at the doorway as if to make certain his woman wasn't listening as he confided in a softer tone, "More than one of the other stockmen in these parts has sort of raised the question of a vigilance committee."

Longarm frowned sternly and warned, "You know how real lawmen feel about vigilantes, Jeff. Private citizens ain't supposed to take the law in their own hands."

Jeff Wade shrugged and morosely replied, "Sometime they have to, when you paid-up lawmen don't seem to give a shit about a bully riding roughshod over 'em and laughing about it. I told the boys I thought we ought to see if we could get you paid-up lawmen to settle Albright's hash before we rode against him less formal."

Then he blew smoke out both nostrils and added, "Christ knows how they're going to take it when I have to tell 'em you said you'd as soon build me a windmill!"

Chapter 5

Less than an hour later, as Longarm had promised, they'd fixed Lucinda Fuller up with a high-stepping cordovan Morgan to ride and the hand called Diego to escort her safely as far as her sister's. He would then come back with both the borrowed pony and her hired sidesaddle. Longarm assured her he'd be proud to drop it off for her at that livery in Aurora, along with a piece of his mind about spavined nags, seeing he'd be heading back sooner.

There'd been no way for them to kiss as hard as they'd felt like as he'd helped her mount up. She'd been a tad put out by his staying behind to drill wells and such. But he'd promised they'd make up for it once he'd paid his own visit, seeing he had her address back in Aurora and all.

Cindy and the cheerful young Mexican hadn't been gone long before Longarm, Jeff, and the other hand called Skinny were putting up the tripod framework you start a tube well with. Skinny was actually a sort of short and thickset young cuss whose real name seemed to be Ekuskin Pryor. He said it was his mama who'd been Arapaho, and that he was used to being called Skinny since he'd been raised Ksiksinum.

Longarm had to think twice before he realized the breed hadn't had another version of his first name in mind. The Arapaho were respected by other Indians as the Grandfather People who'd been out this way hunting buffalo on foot before the invention of the Horse Indian. So they naturally didn't talk the same lingo as the more famous Lakota and·such, though Cheyenne could understand them about as well as a plain American could follow the drift of a Scotsman. Arapaho called white folks Ksiksinum instead of Wasichu. Either term might be translated better as "American" because that stuff Fenimore Cooper had written about "palefaces" didn't quite reflect the way Indians felt about such matters. Arapaho said *ponokahmeta* where a Lakota would say *tashunks* for a pony, *Ma'tou* where a Lakota might say *Wakan Tanka* or *Wakanla* for Great Medicine or Mystery, and so forth. But since Skinny spoke plain Ksiksinum with no accent at all, Longarm didn't bother trying to remember more than that about Quill Indians you didn't see much of in these parts anymore.

The advantage of drilling a tube well was the digging and shoring it saved in soft ground. Once the three of them put up the framework, a sort of skinny guillotine braced solidly on wide-spread legs, you fixed what looked like a couple of yards of pipe with a pointed end and holes drilled through its sides to pound straight down into the prairie loam with a small pile driver powered by a hand line. The wanging and clanging set yard stock to squealing, but the two delighted children came running out to ask if they could help.

They let Judy and Sonny take turns jerking the loose end of the line as they in turn really hoisted and dropped the twelve-pound driver. It drove swell. They'd already screwed on three extra fathoms of tubing, and were fixing to attach and drive another, when two more gents rode in to join them, dismounting from lathered ponies and not offering to help with the rig as one yelled, "Duke Albright's on the warpath,

Wade! Says somebody cut some wire on him and he's mad as hell!"

Jeff introduced Longarm to the gray-bearded Seth Mathis and his grown son, Shem. As they shook hands, Longarm allowed he might be the one who'd cut the wire in question if some damned fool had strung wire across a federal post road.

Seth Mathis pointed off to the northwest, as Longarm had been worried he might. "That's the claim, sure as sin! Duke's chuck wagon driver, Kansas Ferguson, just filed and fenced it in a few days ago."

To which Longarm replied, "No, he never did. Anyone saying he filed a homestead claim smack across a public right-of-way is a man in need of glasses if he ain't an outright liar. When you go to the land office they show you a government plat. That's a large-scale map of, say, a township area, six miles by six, with as many quarter sections as possible laid out to fit the lay of the land best. You got to pick a square they've surveyed with a view to avoiding such mistakes as fences across wagon traces, railroads, and such. You don't get to just claim any old ways."

Jeff Wade thought this over. "By gum, he's right. When I chose this claim I asked if I could sort of swivel it a tad so's I'd have one corner down in that branchwater, with the rest up here higher and drier. They said no dice. I could claim a quarter section with a quarter to a third down in that soggy draw, or I could settle this one, with my boundary lines running along the compass cardinals as they had them on that plat Custis just mentioned!"

Longarm said, "They've been known to make adjustments in mountain country, along serious rivers, and such. But like I just said, no homesteader born of mortal woman could get them to let him block a federal post road, and even if they would, you say this jasper with so much bobwire wrapped around nothing at all drives a chuck wagon for a living?"

46

Jeff Wade snorted in disgust. "I can answer that. My new next-door neighbors are in-laws or hired help of Albright's. Maybe both. Can't you get it through your head the rascal's just being mean, Custis?"

Longarm was about to say it was starting to look that way when the Arapaho breed beside him pointed and gasped, "That's Diego's roan! Coming in without Diego like it's being chased by hornets!"

As the young breed ran to head off and steady the panic-stricken cow pony, Jeff Wade observed, "Something bad must have happened. Diego don't spill easy, and that Morgan we just put your Miss Cindy aboard knows its way home just as well."

The four of them moved as one toward Skinny as the breed got the missing rider's mount under control. As they approached, Skinny declared, "There's blood down the off-fender of Diego's saddle. His pony ain't hit. So *he* must have been."

Jeff Wade gasped, "Jesus, we'd best all saddle up and ride if we're to save that poor gal he was escorting home!"

But Longarm said, "Miss Cindy ain't the only gal to be worried about in these parts, Jeff. You got your wife and kids to guard from whatever's still out there. This highly inflammable spread could be their real target. So you Mathis gents better stay here as well. I brung Miss Cindy this far. So it's my job to go see what can still be done for her."

Skinny said, "Come on. I'll saddle ponies for the two of us, and before you say anything dumb I know the range to the south. You don't. Have I spoken?"

To which Longarm could only reply, "You surely have, old son. So why are we still jawing when the both of us ought to be riding?"

Chapter 6

Longarm figured Jeff knew his own riding stock. So he let Jeff and Skinny rope and bridle a buckskin mare for him while he got his McClellan from the wagon box. Skinny chose a black and white paint to throw his own double-rigged stock saddle aboard. Longarm noticed the breed's saddle gun was a seven-shot Spencer. He didn't ask whether the kid's mom or pop had taught him to shoot. Lots of old-time plainsmen, red or white, cottoned to the slightly outdated Spencer because it flung fewer but bigger .52-caliber slugs. Old Chris Spencer, the Connecticut Yankee who'd invented the weapon back in '60, had been driving a steam-powered horseless carriage to work in '62, when the worried townsfolk had petitioned to keep such a frightening contraption the hell off the roads. Longarm didn't ask Skinny if he was any good with such a husky saddle gun. He'd seldom met any rider who bragged on being a poor shot, and farther along, as the old hymn said, they'd know more about it.

They rode out to the south-southeast toward the county seat at Kiowa with both their saddle guns booted for the first three miles. Then they saw carrion crows rising from the side of the road ahead, and got the guns out as they reined in, as close as you could ask your average cow pony to get near fresh-spilt blood.

The young Mexican called Diego lay half hidden in shin-deep soap-weed just west of the wagon ruts. The crows had been at the bullet hole in his left side as well as his eyes. His hat lay upside down in the grass a few yards on. His boots were missing, and the insides of his pockets stuck out like dusty gray tongues. Skinny said he'd strapped on a Remington .36-30 before mounting up to carry Miss Cindy home. Longarm said he'd noticed. There was no mystery as to where Diego's side arm might have gone. But Longarm wasn't as certain as Skinny he knew the killer's exact name.

Longarm pointed at a trampled clump of prickle poppy a rod off the wagon trace. "Thanks to that recent wet spell we may not have to guess too long at who I'm after. Somebody rode that way at a dead run. A pony won't just stroll through prickle poppy given a choice in the matter."

He heeled his borrowed buckskin in the same direction, figuring Skinny would want to do something about his dead pal. But the breed rode after him, demanding, "What's your hurry? I doubt they really kept going that way. I suspect I *know* where they headed."

Longarm started to suggest Skinny just show him. Then more crows out ahead showed him where he really didn't want to go, but had to just the same.

They found Lucinda Fuller on the far side of the rise. Nobody had shot her. The signs read she'd been roped or just wrestled from that sidesaddle and been spread out on the grass on her back with her brown skirts up around her bare belly. Then she'd had her throat cut, most likely after the last of them had come in her. The carrion crows had been at her down there as well as around her eyes by now.

Longarm swallowed hard, turned in the saddle, and told Skinny to ride back and get some help with both bodies. He added, "I'd like to stay and help. We can't just leave 'em out here like so. But I got to ride on whilst the trail's still fresh."

Skinny said, "They'll kill you, just like they killed Diego back yonder, if you ride on alone. Diego knew this range and they still got the drop on him. I know you're supposed to be good. The boss keeps telling us. But you don't have eyes in the back of your head any more than Diego did!"

Longarm shrugged. "I got an edge old Diego never had. I know they're out here somewheres. He was doubtless just jawing along on a sunny greenup day with a pretty lady. So I'll be on my way now."

Skinny pointed the muzzle of his Spencer another direction entirely as he protested, "Not that way. *This* way. I know why you think they rode west-northwest. I can read sign too. But there's no place to hole up that way. I think they'll make for the old Brandon soddy, more to the southwest. It's been abandoned over a year. They got grasshoppered and tick-fevered out the summer before last. But the soddy still has most of its roof, there's a water hole nearby, and there's nobody with kids within a dozen miles of the place."

Longarm nodded as he stared soberly down at the ghastly sight he'd made love to that very morning. He'd learned in his boyhood, at a place called Shiloh, that they took on that waxy pallor sooner if they'd bled to death. He knew those shapely naked thighs, so warm and alive that morning, would go all sorts of uglier colors as her belly bloated if they didn't get her to an undertaker pronto. So he said, "I got it. Deserted soddy over that way. Thanks for the tip, and I'll put a couple of rounds in 'em for Diego whilst I'm at it."

The breed smiled thinly and said, "I was afraid you were one of those sissies who worried about bringing the sons of bitches back alive."

"Sometimes I do," Longarm said. "I know I'm supposed to. But right now I'm mad as hell, and calling anyone who'd treat a lady like that a son of a bitch would be to flatter him way beyond reason!"

Then he whirled his mount and lit out, loping and cussing for a couple of furlongs while a small grown-up voice inside him told him blind rage was the mark of a frustrated child, a helpless female, or a hireling who went home and beat his woman after kissing a boss's ass all day without being able to do anything about it.

A real man *did* something about it. So he slowed to a mile-eating trot, and reined his temper to a colder resolve while he was at it.

Since a range rider who knew this range better had suggested the sensible way to ride, Longarm only had to stand in the stirrups atop a couple of rises before he was pretty certain that that heavy smoke he and Cindy had spied that morning had been occasioned by somebody trying to dry out an old soddy after all the wet weather. Sod walls held heat or cold way longer than frame or even log walls. He knew a half-ruined soddy that had been exposed to the recent winter with no internal heat at all would need lots of heat to dry out.

It wasn't as clear why the killers had been holing up in such an out-of-the-way place. The easy answer that had ridden in with Seth Mathis and his son didn't explain what someone had been doing in an abandoned soddy long before anyone could have been making war talk about bobwire that hadn't been cut yet.

As he rode on, trying to stay off the skyline as much as he could manage, his primed Winchester on safe but across his thighs with a finger on its trigger, Longarm told the buckskin, "Somebody knowing they'd strung wire smack across a post road would surely be expecting somebody else to come along and cut it."

But he didn't need a talking horse to punch the holes in *that* easy answer. Jeff had said, and Longarm was starting to agree, that Duke Albright seemed a mule-headed bully spoiling for a fight. But would even someone crazy-mean as the Thompson brothers set up a bobwire spiderweb for anybody going either way along that post road?

"Why lay for such a victim in an abandoned soddy, then advertise a pending showdown over a fence you just knew somebody was going to have to cut? If a chuck-wagon driver on Albright's payroll fenced that quarter section, accidental or on purpose, why would he or the boss who put him up to it spend last night trying to dry out that abandoned soddy? Doesn't Duke Albright have any permanent address with doors, windows, and a solid roof?"

As he made out what could have been the remains of another bobwire fence along the rise ahead, Longarm reined in, muttering, "I reckon I might want to take at least one of 'em alive, for a few minutes leastways. For I'm missing something about all this shit, and it's funny how helpful some suspects can be when you sit on their chest with a six-gun in one hand and a barlow knife in the other."

As he drifted westward in line with that rusted-out or salvaged fence line, the sky assured him the remaining posts ran more due east and west than anything but a boundary fence needed to. He knew he'd guessed right when he ran out of fence posts in the middle of nowhere, eased up the slope a ways, and saw that, sure enough, other posts ran due south around what had to be the corner of somebody's abandoned claim line.

He worked his way a few furlongs farther west, so he could ride below the skyline for a while. Then he reined in, dismounted with his Winchester, and tethered the buckskin to a fresh green tumbleweed.

Tumbleweed stays put, on stout tap roots, till it sets seeds, dries out, and busts off at the root-crown to wander the world scattering itself.

There was more of the stuff, green and still graze-worthy, or dried out and detached, as Longarm eased up to that row of posts and wisps of rusty wire in an ever-lower crouch. He crawled the last few yards with his Winchester riding the crooks of his elbows, and then he saw he'd judged the usual layout about right. He'd hit the fence line midway along its half-mile length. The old soddy Skinny had told him about squatted down near the southwest corner of the abandoned claim. The native short-grass and a few exotic weeds had reclaimed such sod as had ever been busted.

Longarm didn't care about that. The thing he liked was the ruined sod stable and what seemed an old frame shit-house between him and any back windows of the main house. He worked back down to his borrowed buckskin and regathered the reins, leading it afoot as he confided, "I'm fixing to see if I can work close enough to their back wall without being spotted, for some more foolish but fairly short charging."

The pony didn't seem to care. This time he tethered it to some soap-weed, loosely so it wouldn't starve to death out here if something happened.

But nobody shot him as he worked his way in close and then just strode up to the back door, Winchester aimed the same way from the hip, and simply kicked it in, yelling, "Grab some sky and don't move an eyelash!" Then he tore inside and shot a dark form dead center before he realized it was a man-sized damp streak down a wall that was more mustard-tan everywhere else.

There was nothing else to shoot at. But you could still smell the kindling and cow chips someone had burned in there fairly recently. A cigar butt on the packed dirt floor looked fresh as well.

He was still rummaging around, trying to read such little sign as they'd left, when he heard hoofbeats and eased over to a gaping window to spy Skinny Pryor riding in. As he stepped outside the breed called out, "What happened? I heard gunshots!"

Longarm said, "You heard *one*. That was me, spooked by a blotch on 'dobe-plastered sod. You were right about somebody holed up here a short spell back. But they ain't here now, and I'm open to suggestions as to where we cut their damn trail again!"

Skinny started to explain how he'd fetched the Mathis boy and old Jeff's buckboard for Diego and Miss Cindy. But Longarm snapped, "That's what I told you to do. Never mind about them. We were talking about their killers. They ain't here. So they must be somewheres else!"

Skinny nodded soberly and said, "Ten to one they've made it back to the Albright home spread by this time. We'd better ride on into the county seat and talk about all this with the sheriff. Duke Albright's big sod castle is too big for just the two of us, Longarm. I ain't sure the sheriff and a posse could take the place by storm if Duke means to make a fight of it. But he might not want to shoot it out with both county and federal law unless he really has to."

Longarm started to object. But the young breed's words made a heap of sense. So he nodded and replied, "Let's try her your way. You think the sheriff will side with us instead of your local cattle baron, Skinny?"

The cowhand grimaced and said, "Albright ain't a cattle baron yet. He just thinks he is. He's got a heap of hired help and even more money. But there's more voting men in this county who hate his guts, and the sheriff likely knows that."

Skinny started to dismount. Longarm said, "Stay in the saddle. I left that buckskin just the other side of yonder shithouse, and if your sheriff ain't interested in the next election I might be able to convince him he still ought to side with Uncle Sam. For as Robert E. Lee kept saying to the last, nobody but a sucker wants to a fight with the U.S. of A."

Skinny smiled thinly. "If you say so. Haven't some of my mother's nation stood up to you boys since Robert E. surrendered?"

Longarm smiled right back. "Some of *my* mother's people too. Ain't none of 'em *won* yet."

Chapter 7

There was little profit in scouting for more sign once it was clear nobody had been in those parts since before the killings. Skinny suggested, and Longarm agreed, they'd make better time to the county seat if they cut back over to the post road. Roads were laid out cross-country with easy going in mind.

They naturally rode catty-corner toward the road to Kiowa, and as he spied a sod roof more to their left Longarm said, "Oh, Lord, I hope that ain't where Miss Cindy's sister lives. I mean to pay my respects as soon as I've got more time, but . . ."

"That's the Tuttle spread," Skinny said. "You told old Diego to carry her to the Davis place, right?"

Longarm agreed, mighty relieved, and once they were back on the road things got even better. Skinny said they'd overshot Cindy's kin, and that Jeff Wade had said he'd store both bodies in the root cellar while he sent to town for the country coroner.

Skinny added, "Boss says you ain't supposed to mess with dead folk more than you need to before the coroner looks 'em over and says it's all right to hand 'em over to the undertaker. Ksiksinum sure take a dead body serious. My mom's folk used to just lay 'em out under the sky on some windswept rise. Seems way neater to me."

Longarm started to observe the breed had likely never camped downwind of a platform burial by mistake. But he didn't want to think of good old Cindy smelling like that, above or below the ground. So to change the subject, he pointed down the road ahead and asked whose homestead that was off to their right.

Skinny said, "Old Man Wurtz and his two grown daughters, or so he says. Some say he's a secret Mormon. You want to question them? I mean about them other riders, not whether they're secret Mormons."

Longarm chuckled and replied, "I doubt we'd get answers we could use on either subject. This is a public thoroughfare and we have no idea what those killers look like, or even how many of them there may be. So what would be the point in asking folks along the side of this road if they've seen anyone else ride by, aside from wasting time, I mean."

Skinny agreed, and they would have ridden right on by, despite a gal waving at them as she went on hanging laundry out back. But then Longarm noticed the ponies in the pole corral behind her and asked Skinny, "Wasn't that a cordovan Morgan you all saddled up for Miss Cindy to ride to her sister's?"

The younger cowhand nodded, blinked owlishly at the riding stock on the far side of that laundry-hanging gal, and decided, "No doubt about it! That's old Dusty sure as hell!"

So they reined into the Wurtz dooryard slow and thoughtful, as an old gent with a long ginger beard and another young gal in a flour-sack shift and bare feet came out of their soddy unarmed, which was just as well for the both of them.

Old Man Wurtz naturally knew Skinny, and said so friendly enough. The breed introduced Longarm, who got right down

57

to brass tacks by asking, "Where did you get that cordovan Morgan out back?"

The older man looked easy in his own mind as he replied without hesitation, "Thought them boys were in too much of a hurry for honest strangers. Told Emma and Daisy as much at the time."

"Time is what we're running low on," Longarm snapped, not trying to sound polite. "Get to the point. We're trailing a bunch of killers and we ain't got time for small talk!"

The older man exchanged glances with Emma, or Daisy, and then he told Longarm, "You're trailing three, you mean. Never seen any of 'em in these parts afore. Looked like saddle tramps of average ragged-ass appearance. You missed 'em by, say, two hours ago. They rode in aboard three jaded ponies and leading the Morgan you just mentioned. Said they had to make it into Kiowa in time to meet the afternoon stage. Offered to swap us four jaded ponies for three fresh ones, no money changing hands. We naturally took 'em up on it. Ain't often a man has such an easy chance to come out a pony ahead!"

Skinny shook his head and said, "No, you didn't. Don't know who the other three might belong to, but old Dusty belongs to Jeff Wade, and they hang horse thieves in Colorado!"

Longarm said calmly, "The man just said he came by that Morgan in what he took to be an honest transaction, and we can worry about old Dusty later. Somebody mentioned something about an afternoon stage?"

Skinny said, "Overland feeder line. Runs every other day to the railroad stop at Peyton. Now that you call it to mind, I reckon it will be passing through Kiowa today. More like this evening than this afternoon, though. Stage crew generally has supper in Kiowa before they make the night run down to the Arkansas Divide."

Longarm said, "It's about time things started going our way!"

Then he turned to the old nester to ask for a description of those three ponies.

Old Man Wurtz said he'd swapped them a chestnut with white stockings, a strawberry roan, and another cordovan, that one a jug-headed Indian pony. Only the chestnut, an old army gelding the remount service had sold off as lamed, wore a brand.

When Longarm observed there were lots of eldery chestnuts branded U.S., the Arapaho breed beside him said, "I think I know that dusky jug-headed Indian pony on sight."

He turned back to Old Man Wurtz. "Wasn't that one a true *ponokahmeta* my mother's people called Stamix Otokan, and didn't you buy him off the widow of old Charley Kyi-Yo-Kosi cheap after he died of the cholera last summer?"

Old Man Wurtz shrugged and muttered, "A man buys cheap and sells dear if he's got a lick of sense. Has anybody said I cheated anybody?"

Longarm cut the discussion short by telling Skinny, "Forget where that jug-head might have come from and let's see if we can find out where it went!"

So they rode on faster, and it didn't take them all that long to make the trail town and county seat of Kiowa.

After you called it a county seat, there wasn't a whole lot more you could say about the dinky town. Kiowa hunkered mostly on the east bank of the Kiowa Creek it was named after, or vice versa, which ran due north across the rolling prairie to the more serious South Platte. The town consisted of forty or fifty private homes wrapped around a crossroads business and courthouse hub. A town of, say, three hundred permanent residents with thrice that number on payday got to be the seat of its fair-sized county because it was still bigger than any of the other eight or ten settlements scattered off across the surrounding High Plains, most of which was still open range.

First things coming first, Longarm and Skinny reined in across from the Overland stop and only hotel in town to ask about anyone else who'd been asking about that evening stage to Peyton. Half a dozen local folks had. Four of them wanted to ride down to catch them a train ride. But none of them had been strangers in the company of any sort of horseflesh.

Longarm's next call was naturally on the county law. Sheriff Mike Otis had his combined office and county lockup around back of the white-frame courthouse. Longarm would have had to look harder for it if Skinny hadn't been along. It was the local cowhand who recognized those other ponies tethered out front. So neither he nor Longarm was all that surprised when they found Jeff Wade and young Shem Mathis in the front office with Sheriff Otis and his two deputies.

Jeff said the older Mathis and some other neighbors had things under control out to his spread. So he and Shem had come into town to report the killings and swear out a warrant against that son of a bitch Duke Albright.

Sheriff Otis, a lean and hungry man of about fifty, with a mustache that would have done a Chinee mandarin proud, got up from his desk to shake Longarm's hand and say it was an honor. He then agreed it had been mean as hell to gun that Mexican and murder that Fuller gal, but said that he didn't see how he could arrest Duke Albright on either charge.

Longarm said, "Miss Cindy wasn't just murdered. We found her out there after the three of them had raped her and slit her throat. But I never said this Duke Albright did it. I want to ask him why he *told* somebody to do it, assuming he did."

Otis shook his grizzled head and objected. "He couldn't have. He wasn't in position to order anybody to do anything this morning. I keep telling these other gents, whether they want to listen or not, I met Albright and his head lawyer, Rathbone, having dinner at the Lovelace House around noon. They'd just come up from Pueblo Town, they said. So how could—"

"Anyone can *say* he spent the morning most anywheres!" Jeff Wade shouted "Would it be too much to ask you to wire Pueblo and check that mighty handy alibi, Sheriff?"

Otis shrugged and calmly replied, "I'd be willing, if you'd care to pay and had the least notion who to wire down that way. No offense, but I just can't see wiring hither and yon at the county's expense to prove nothing. I follow your drift, Mister Wade, but you couldn't prove you were in Kiowa today just by wiring the Lovelace House or First Methodist Manse to ask if they'd seen you here today."

Seth Mathis started to cuss. Sheriff Otis said, "Watch your mouth. I got my wife's tintype on my desk. Albright and his lawyer say they were in Pueblo Town to visit another lawyer on business. So what good would it do if no barkeep or whore down yonder would back their story, if they produced one business associate who would?"

Longarm said, "I ain't after any of Albright's business associates in Pueblo yet. I want to talk to him about those three sons of bitches we trailed as far as the Wurtz spread and then lost. Skinny here says Albright's forted up in a big sod castle with a sort of private army. That's how he persuaded me to call on you for help before I ride out that way to grill Albright about his surly war talk just before two folks aboard Wade riding stock were killed!"

Seth Mathis said, "Damned right. Are you fixing to do your duty and posse up? Or would you rather we round up our own pals to ride out there informal?"

Otis smiled thinly, looking as mandarin as any Chinese as he told the bearded Mathis, "Nobody has to do neither. Duke Albright won't be out at his home spread this afternoon. He'll be over in the courthouse with Lawyer Rathbone getting sued some more. Silas Dorman's taking Albright to court over access rights. Seems some of Duke's hands dug an irrigation ditch and strung four strands of Glidden Brand right across Dorman's driveway out to the post road. Ain't that a bitch?"

Jeff Wade frowned thoughtfully and told Longarm, "I know where Lawyer Rathbone's office is, Custis. If they're not at the courthouse, they'll likely be hanging around over yonder."

Longarm grimaced and replied, "I'd rather talk to three other suspects first. They were last seen headed this way on an old army chestnut, a strawberry roan, and a jug-headed Indian pony. I've yet to see any stock like that tethered anywhere along the streets of Kiowa. But you do have a town corral and livery, don't you?"

Sheriff Otis said, "Sure we do. I'll have my boys show you the way."

Skinny said, "I know the way. I know the pony called Stamix Otokan when I see him too. Let's go, Longarm. Diego was a pal of mine!"

Chapter 8

The fat full-blood in charge of the town corral seemed to feel more at ease talking to Skinny in Arapaho. Longarm let them, once he'd spotted that strawberry roan and Skinny had identified the smaller dusky jug-head in the corral as the Indian pony he knew on sight. There was more than one chestnut wearing an old cavalry brand amid the two dozen head out yonder in the corral. The remount service tended to sell off stock that looked or acted sickly cheap. It saved the army a lot of horse-doctoring, and offered a sporting man a chance to pick up a fair mount at a good price—or a hide and a lot of dog food at a poor price if he'd guessed wrong on how much care and rest an over-the-hill cavalry brute needed to bounce back.

Arapaho was even tougher to follow on the fly than Lakota or Shoshoni, which may have been why sign lingo had been invented for all Horse Indians to use. The nice thing about talking to an Indian with your hands, once you learned how to do it, was how the hand motion conveyed the meaning of your message no matter what words you or the other cuss spoke out loud. When you made the sign of cutting your fingers, any Horse Indian knew which nation you were asking about, whether he called them Tsitsissah or Cheyenne. A stiff palm held above one's eyes, like a painted Indian peering off at covered wagons, or like the brim of cavalry hat, meant the two of you were talking about white men, whether you called them Wasichu, Saltu, or Ksiksinum. So Longarm horned into the conversation with hand talk as well as the English any hostler had to savvy if he wanted to run a damned town corral, and the full-blood repeated what Skinny had just translated about only two riders coming in aboard yonder roan and cordovan. Nobody the hostler didn't know had left any of those chestnuts they saw.

Longarm said aloud, "They must have split up before they got to town. Or mayhaps the one riding the chestnut didn't think he had as much to worry about. It's safe to assume that at least two of them have to be here in Kiowa fixing to board that stage."

Then he sighed and added, "Unless they lied about that too. A man who'd rape a lady and slit her throat might not balk at fibbing about his intended destination."

Skinny volunteered, "There ain't but half a dozen houses of ill repute and them few saloons along Main Street."

Longarm grimaced. "Swell. You take one side and I'll take the other as we ask total strangers to tell us whether they've been out killing folks this afternoon."

He turned back to the full-blood to question him in sign about the details of the two strange riders' outfits. The Indian replied in English, "Jesus Christ, your sign is no better than my American! As I told the boy here, they were both about the same height. Taller than me. Shorter than you. Maybe my age. Not any younger than you. Dusty jeans, one gray shirt. One army shirt. An old one. Sun-faded, with a couple of brass buttons pearl, now. Both had dusty gray hats. Both carried their saddle guns from the tack room after I showed them where to leave their saddles. They had no rolls or saddlebags.

But I can show you the saddles they rode in on."

Longarm frowned thoughtfully and decided, "Man who don't leave nothing on a likely begged or borrowed saddle ain't likely to leave a home address pasted to it. You say they both packed saddle guns, not pistols?"

The Indian nodded. "Wait. One had a six-gun riding low on his left hip. Ivory grips. Gun rig was black, tooled, and mounted with German silver, I think."

Skinny gasped. "That sounds like Diego's Remington the son of a bitch is wearing now!"

Longarm nodded soberly. "Might be the break we needed. I see plain-looking cowhands all over cow country, but not too many of 'em packing an ivory-gripped Remington in a tooled Mexican rig. You say they have both saloons and whore houses open in broad day around here, Skinny?"

The cowhand shrugged. "Hell, it's the county seat, ain't it? Why don't we start with Madame Fitzroy's, up at the north end?"

But Longarm had a better notion. He'd done this chore before. It was part of his trade to guess the most likely place a man on the dodge might hole up. So he suggested they leave their own mounts at the town corral and mosey over to that stage stop some more.

Skinny said he didn't mind hunting on foot, but pointed out they'd already talked to the Overland agent at that hotel.

Longarm waited until they'd stored their saddles in the tack room and stepped back out in the sunlight with their carbines to explain in more detail. "We often get a tip some cuss means to get out of town by rail or stage. Half the time it's a false lead. A third of the others are caught hanging about the stage stop or railroad depot, like big-ass birds, before it's time to get aboard. Another third hole up clear out of range, and you only catch 'em when and if they make a last-minute run for it. That leaves the third who don't want to be spotted waiting and don't want to have to run for it. They usually find a nearby hidey-hole with a window they can watch the stop or depot from. So seeing you know this town best, Skinny, where would you while away the afternoon, off the streets but still able to see what's going on around that Overland stop?"

Since the two of them were headed that way by then, Skinny felt no call to point down the street as he said, "I'd likely book me a room in that hotel, with a window overlooking the front walk!"

Longarm smiled thinly and said, "Close, but no cigar. With all due respect to your prairie metropolis, Skinny, a two-story hotel a stranger would have to register in to get upstairs ain't my notion of an impenetrable maze. The saloon I recall just across the way seems an obvious place for us to check."

Skinny nodded, shifted his Spencer to port arms, and said, "Let's go check it then. You want me to go round to the alley exit whilst you move in from the street?"

Longarm shook his head. "Not hardly. I just said it was obvious. I never said killers on the run would be standing out like sore thumbs in a neighborhood saloon on a workday. But I did see a schoolyard, and wasn't that a public library just this side of the business center?"

Skinny thought, shrugged, and replied, "That might be a library betwixt the schoolyard and the stage stop. To tell the truth, I've never paid much mind to schools and such since I got big enough to lick the truant officer back home."

Longarm said, "I left school early to attend a war one time. But I like libraries more ways than one. Aside from borrowing books to read when I'm low on pocket jingle, I've noticed a lot of owlhoot trail riders take out library cards as they wander about. Somebody must teach them that trick in prison, judging by the numbers who've been found dead or alive with library cards made out to John Doe or Richard Roe. Anyways, knowing how many roving crooks know libraries make good temporary hideouts, and knowing there's a library less than two hundred yards from that stage stop, I reckon I'll just go see if they have the latest edition of the *Police Gazette* in their reading room."

Chapter 9

But that failed to pan out. The mousy little librarian had the *Police Gazette* and *Scientific American* on hand, but the only other souls in her reading room were an old gent in a rusty suit and an even older lady reading a book about pet birds. Skinny was too polite to laugh as they stepped back out on the steps of the modest frame building. But he did ask where Longarm meant to look next.

Longarm shrugged and said, "Outlaws on the run *have* been known to while away their remaining moments in a neighborhood saloon. I don't want you acting heroic in any alley with that Spencer, though. If they're there they're experienced killers and, no offense, Jeff hired you and Diego for less exciting chores."

Skinny asked if he could at least back Longarm's play as he led the way in via the back door. Longarm had just said he could when the local rider murmured, "Speaking of sneaky rascals, yonder comes a brace of 'em!"

Longarm followed the breed's gaze, regarded the dapper gent in a summer-weight dove-gray frock coat and the husky cuss dressed more like a mighty prosperous cow hand, and asked soberly, "Might the one in the sissy outfit be the law-yer?"

Skinny said, "Yep, Lawyer Rathbone. Guess who the bully in the tailored riding duds and two six-guns has to be. The sheriff said Silas Dorman was taking Albright to court this afternoon, and that's where they're likely headed now."

Longarm put a hand on the breed's sleeve. "Let them head wherever they like. Do you know where that dapper lawyer's office might be, Skinny?"

The breed nodded. "Sure I do. Just down the other side of the stage depot. But Rathbone won't be there when you can see him in plain view across the . . . Oh, I follow your drift!"

So Longarm followed Skinny, along the alley running behind the business block across from the hotel and stage stop, until, a few minutes later, they were standing in the shadows of the stairway running up the side of a frame building to the second story.

Longarm told the young breed, "Stay here and see no inno-cent or guilty bystanders head up them stairs after me. I'll go see what I can see. You're sure Rathbone's office is down at the far end once I make her to the top of the stairs?"

Skinny said, "Don't know the room number. But he's got his name on the door in gilt lettering."

Longarm nodded, repeated his instructions to stay put, and eased out of the slot between buildings to head up the stairs, telling the big green cat in his stomach to quit swishing its fuzzy tail like that, damn it.

A million years later he was all the way up and still alive. So he opened the door and started to step into the dark sec-ond story.

Then, down below, he heard Skinny yelling something as a gun went off too close for comfort and a slug spanged off the doorjamb near his head.

As Skinny, or somebody, fired round after round and cussed

like hell downstairs, Longarm dove forward into the tricky light of the windowless hallway.

He was glad he'd come in fast and low when another gun blazed in the gloom down the hall to envelop him in black-powder smoke and repeated ear-splitting roars as he belly-flopped to the floor and fired back with his Winchester until he heard somebody yell, "I give up! I give up! You got me bad and I need me a doc!"

Longarm fired at the sound of the other cuss on the floor, and grunted in satisfaction as he heard somebody scream like a coyote giving birth to a litter of busted bottles. For whether the jasper had been sincere or not, Cindy had been a pretty little thing.

It got quiet for a spell as Longarm just lay there, waiting for the smoke to clear. Behind him, he heard Skinny Pryor calling out to him. He called back, "I'm all right. Think I got at least one of 'em. Who were you shooting at just now?"

He heard boots coming up the stairs. More than one pair. But the young breed was the one who called back. "Never seen him before. He come out of nowheres and throwed down on you just as you was opening this here door. Is it safe for us to open it some more now?"

Longarm hadn't noticed it swinging shut on its sprung hinges. He glanced the other way to make out the soles of two boots in the smoke haze. One toe was twitching like the tail of a stomped-dead sidewinder. He yelled for Skinny to hold the thought as he rose to his knees and one hand for a better look. Easing forward, he saw he'd hit the jasper in the chest and groin, likely in that order.

He called, "I got the one up here. You say you got another?"

Skinny opened the door from outside cautiously as he replied, "Not hardly. I pegged a shot at him as he was pegging a shot at you and we both missed. He ran out the other end of the slot, onto the street, I reckon."

The townsman right behind the breed volunteered, "Must have ducked into some doorway sudden. I was on the walk across the way when I heard the gunplay and came a-running, being the town marshal. You say you shot somebody up here, mister? I sure hope you have a good excuse."

Skinny said, "He's the law. The famous federal man they call Longarm."

So the local lawman asked if there was anything he could do to help.

Longarm felt the throat of the one he'd downed as he replied in a disgusted voice, "You can help me get this one over to the county coroner's. Now that I've played the fool, I'm sorry I didn't listen when he allowed I'd already hit him serious enough. He might have had more to say. But I was het up to begin with, and he didn't seem to be suffering in a convincing manner."

Longarm picked up the twitching dead man's Henry carbine and got to his feet. "This wasn't the one wearing Diego's gun. I'd say he was a professional with some prison-time education on the art of being taken for a saddle tramp by small-town law, no offense."

The local lawman, younger than Longarm had first expected as he'd come down the hall through the clearing smoke, bent over the man on the hall runner for a closer look, shook his head, and said, "Never seen him in these parts before. But you were right about him looking like a saddle tramp. What do you gents reckon he was doing up here?"

Longarm answered dryly, "Visiting his lawyer most likely. I've been given to understand that's Lawyer Rathbone's office down at the far end."

The town law replied, "It surely is. Only Rathbone's supposed to be in court this afternoon representing another client. You saying this other one came outten Rathbone's office?"

Longarm nodded, but then he muttered, "Hold it," as he

stepped around the body and moved down the hall, reloading his saddle gun while he was at it.

The office door at the far end was paneled solid and lettered in gilt as Skinny had suggested. It seemed to be locked on the inside. As Longarm knocked with the muzzle of his Winchester, the town law said, "Old Rathbone's secretary gal will have preceded him to the courthouse to parley with the country clerk, take notes, and such. Ain't nobody in there now."

Longarm fished out a pocketknife and growled, "We'll see about that. You gents stand to one side in case that Remington poor Diego was packing goes off unexpected!"

But it never did. The more brightly illuminated office suite on the far side was really vacant when Longarm finished picking the lock to let the three of them in.

By this time others had crowded into the hallway behind them. So the town law deputized one of the townsmen he knew to clear the rest back as far as the stairs, and asked a young kid to go fetch Doc Miller, the full-time dentist and part-time county coroner.

Longarm had no call to poke about in Lawyer Rathbone's office, even if he'd had a search warrant. So having satisfied himself the place was empty, he herded everyone back outside as he declared, "It works more ways than one. Yonder gun waddy on the floor could have been in Rathbone's office or one of these other whatevers when he heard me on the steps and stepped out to greet me with that dumb fusillade. In any event, he'd have shut the door behind to keep from being outlined by window light. Rathbone's door has a spring latch. What can either of you tell me about these other six doors I can count from right here?"

Skinny said, "That's right! How come nobody's come out of any of these other offices, or even peeked, as noisy as it's been up here for the past few minutes?"

The town law said, "I can answer that. Ain't nobody open

72

for business on this story but Rathbone since Duke Albright bought the building. I heard he'd evicted the realtor and taxidermist who'd hired the two other front offices so's a couple of other law firms could move in. Don't know if they have yet. But like Pryor here just said—"

"What do you suppose they've been keeping behind those three doors along the rear?" Longarm said, trying another latch with his free hand as he palmed the pocketknife.

A strange voice called down the hall. "I can answer that. We mean to use those rooms for storage, and who in blue blazes is this saddle tramp oozing all over my hall runner?"

Longarm calmly regarded the blustering Duke Albright and his small slithery lawyer as they pushed down the hall as far as the corpse as if they owned the place—which they did, as soon as anyone studied on it.

Longarm smiled thinly and replied, "I was hoping you gents could tell me, Mister Albright. I'd be Deputy U.S. Marshal Custis Long, and you see him there because I just shot him. I take it the judge granted the postponement a slick lawyer always cuts the card with?"

Lawyer Rathbone slithered forward between Longarm and his burlier client as he replied with a surprisingly deep tone of authority that *he'd* ask the questions, beginning with how come his office door was open on its hinges after he'd locked it behind him on his way to see the judge.

Longarm pointed at the dead man at their feet with the muzzle of his Winchester, saying, "I had just cause to suspect a confederate of this gunslick might have stayed inside your office when this one popped out of it at me. We know there were three of them. Ekuskin Pryor here only saw one, down them outside stairs of yourn, so—"

"You say this total stranger came out of my office?" Rathbone asked, sounding sincerely puzzled as he shook his head. "Neither I nor my secretary, Miss Redfern, gave anyone permission to use our suite while we were away for the afternoon. Are you certain he came out of my office and not, say, that storage closet to the left of my door?"

Longarm started to say something unprofessional. Then he had to nod grudgingly. "I'll buy that, if you'd like to tell me why a killer on the run would go up to a lawyer's office and wind up in his broom closet!"

Rathbone smiled sincerely as a coyote regarding a newly yeaned range lamb and replied, "I can't tell you anything about him. You were the one who shot him. I've never seen him before."

He turned to Duke Albright to ask, "What about you, Duke? Have you ever seen this poor unfortunate before?"

Albright replied, "Never laid eyes on him afore. Don't look like no gunslick to this child. Where's his *buscadero* six-gun rig if he's supposed to be that sort of cuss?"

Before Longarm had to answer such a stupid question, another new voice called down the hall, "Somebody say a man's been shot up here?"

The town law yelled for the boys at the far end to let their own damned coroner through. So they did. Doc Miller was even taller than Longarm and, like the town law, sort of young-looking for his job. Small communities were like that. Paying country wages, you wound up with young and ambitious or old and worn out.

As the towering county coroner hunkered down for a look-see at the dead man nobody seemed to know, Lawyer Rathbone invited Longarm and the town law to duck into his more spacious office along with his client, Duke Albright. Skinny Pryor tagged along without waiting to be asked.

They were joined within minutes by Doc Miller, who drawled, "He's dead as a turd in a milk bucket with no mystery as to the cause. Would anybody like to give me a name for his death certificate? All I found in his pockets was

74

a snot rag and twenty-two dollars and change."

Longarm got out a cheroot to light up as he tersely filled the county coroner and town law in on all the deaths that afternoon. Doc Miller said he'd heard about the bodies out to the Wade spread, and had sent somebody to haul them into town. Duke Albright and Lawyer Rathbone let on that was the first they'd heard of any other killings. Longarm dryly observed, "I figured Albright here would have a fair alibi for the times in question. You're fixing to assure us your client was here in town with you when others heard him making war talk about that fool fence he strung across a public right of way. And naturally, nobody riding for him was spotted in the company of a dead gal's mount or shot it out in the hall with me just now."

Duke Albright moved over to the window to stare down at the crowd out front as his oily lawyer smiled bold as brass and told Longarm, "You'd best rein in, Deputy. We just told you neither of us had ever seen that dead man in the hall before."

"Then what was he doing up here, with your office the only one on this floor these days?" Longarm demanded.

The lawyer shrugged and replied, "What were *you* doing out in that hall, before you broke into this office without a warrant, I mean?"

Longarm nodded curtly and said, "Fair question. I figured a hired gun on the dodge might ask the ones who hired him to hide him out as long as it took him to catch the next stage out. Do I have to say how I figured who might have hired him and his two pals?"

Lawyer Rathbone turned to the county coroner to say, "You're my witness, Doctor Miller. Seems to me I just heard somebody accuse my client of paying someone to murder and rape a young lady none of us ever laid eyes on, unless he'd like to rephrase his explanation."

Longarm snorted smoke out both nostrils and snapped, "I ain't about to take back shit! Did or did not your client threaten the lives of whoever cut his pesky wire, and did or did not somebody put a rifle ball in Diego Capaz, then rape and murder Lucinda Fuller a few damned minutes later?"

Duke Albright turned from the window to protest, "I never raped nobody! I don't have to! I'm too pretty!"

His lawyer silenced him by snapping, "Let *me* do the talking! I'll have his badge to remember him by if he tries to make such wild accusations stick!"

Turning back to Longarm, the lawyer sneered, "I know what my client said about anyone low enough to cut a fence. I was with him at the time, in the Overland Hotel tap room, when a rider came in to tell us someone had cut through Kansas Ferguson's claim line twice. Neither of us knew it was you who'd done it, of course. You certainly have a crude approach to other people's property lines and locked doors— for a lawman, I mean."

Longarm snorted, "Don't lecture me on common law. I told you I had just cause to make certain nobody was holed up in here with a gun. Your client already knew he'd strung bobwire across a federal post road before it got cut!"

Duke Albright opened his mouth as if to say something. But Rathbone shushed him again and said, "Point one: My client never strung a yard of wire over at Kansas Ferguson's claim. That boundary wire you admit you cut was naturally strung by a part-time employee and personal friend of Mister Albright."

"I heard he paid his hired help a lot," Longarm dryly observed.

The lawyer said, "Point two: *Nobody* ran any wire across any public thoroughfare. Before you say anything else as silly, Ferguson rode in a little while ago to concede somebody seems to have played a malicious trick on him. He says it

76

looks as if some kids moved a good many fence posts on the sly, and so we're willing to concede the whole affair was an honest misunderstanding, occasioned by malicious mischief, if you'd care to agree a man has a right to get upset when he hears some idiot's been running loose with wire cutters!"

Longarm started to say that the notion of somebody shifting a whole quarter-section homestead claim like the pea in that old shell game sounded mighty difficult. But fair was fair, and it wasn't as if he'd seen anything put bobwire around an unproven claim of unplowed and totally natural prairie. So he gripped his cheroot between his bared teeth to reply, "I can check where that wire was meant to be strung with the land office, and you have my word I mean to. *I* got points to make as well, starting with two folks winding up dead right after—"

"My client threatened to clean the plow of the one who cut that wire," Rathbone cut in, adding with an innocent smile, "Haven't you admitted *you* were the one who cut it, and has anyone harmed one hair on *your* chin?"

Longarm scowled and said, "No, but . . ."

"But me no buts and make no charges you don't mean to back up in court!" the lawyer shouted, turning back to the coroner and local law as he continued in a more reasonable tone. "My client and his own associates have nothing to hide. Neither Duke nor Kansas Ferguson was anywhere near the Wade spread this afternoon, and even if they had been, did anybody *see* them attacking those other innocent souls for no reason at all?"

The town law nodded at Longarm and quietly declared, "They say you got to show motive as well as means and opportunity before you charge anyone with any felony, Uncle Sam."

Longarm swore softly and said, "I know. I'm working on it."

Chapter 10

They had a Western Union office in Kiowa to make up for their lack of rail connections to the outside world. So somebody wired the dead Diego's kin down Pikes Peak way when Seth Mathis drove in with the other two bodies. The assistant coroner had allowed it was best to get them both embalmed as soon as possible, with the day turning out so warm in the end. Nobody had to wire Cindy's kin back up the road. Her sister and brother-in-law had said they'd come in later to talk about her funeral. Seth said they'd told the brother-in-law, but not Cindy's sister, why it might be best to wait till she'd been tidied and boxed before they viewed the body.

By this time Longarm had told the tale many times, in writing as well as having to repeat his weary words aloud, and it was getting to where he could have gotten away with calling it a day as shadows lengthened and some started drifting home for a sit-down before supper. But a man who wanted answers kept seeking them as long as anyone would let him, and they'd said the land office stayed open till six.

Kiowa being a dinky rural community, for all its being a county seat, the federal government's few offices there were modest as hell. The post office would have made an average fisherman's cottage out on that Cape Cod the style of white clapboard and shingle roof went with. The federal county agent manned the local office of the Bureau of Land Management in another frame structure smaller than that far-from-grand public library.

But at least the door was unlocked when Longarm tried it. So he went on in. The first soul he saw was a weary-looking ash-blonde in a lemon and lime print dress, seated at a long oak table with a mess of those pasteboard folders they kept survey charts in. When Longarm started to tell her who he was and what he wanted, she told him she was visiting too, and called out a bit louder for somebody else to deal with him.

Another gal, not as young or pretty, came out from the back to favor Longarm with a weary smile and tell him they were fixing to shut down for the day any minute.

He flashed his badge and identification at her as he told her firmly but not unkindly, "I can let myself out when I'm done here, ma'am. I am a federal lawman investigating crimes too numerous to go into yet another time. So suffice it to say, there seems to be some dispute as to where somebody strung bobwire earlier. I'd like to start by comparing the homestead claim of one Kansas Ferguson, if that's his true name, with the official government map of this here county, which would surely be Elbert, in the state of Colorado."

The gal he was talking to looked down at the gal at the table, who declared, "I have what you're looking for right here, Deputy. I was just checking that same claim for my employer, Nathan Rathbone, Esquire."

Longarm blinked, thought, and said, "Then you must be Miss Redfern, his secretary gal."

It had been a statement rather than a question. She still nodded and replied, "Florence Redfern. My friends all call me Flo."

Longarm nodded. "In that case, Miss Florence, you have

to know why I want to see just where Kansas Ferguson was supposed to have strung that bobwire."

The ash-blonde nodded, and swung an open folder around for him to examine just by stepping closer. As he did she said, "His name is really Kansas. He was born there just as his parents arrived by Conestoga wagon thirty-odd years ago. I heard about a federal lawman saying they'd strung wire across that post road. That's why my employer sent me over here this afternoon."

As Longarm bent slightly for a better view of the freshly inked lines on the plat, which was printed in lighter sepia, Flo Redfern told him what he could see with his own eyes. According to the land office and this recorded claim, the Ferguson quarter section lay well off that road to the east. It had been shrewdly chosen, if unwisely fenced. Heaps of homesteaders wound up with a few acres of extra land by claiming within a rod or so of a road and then fencing clean out to it, since nobody else was ever going to be able to use such a narrow misshapen strip.

Longarm nodded grudgingly and said, "Makes more sense that way than a furlong to the west with a road running smack across it. But I know what I was cutting when I cut that bobwire early this very long day."

The weary-looking young blonde agreed it *had* been a long day, but offered no suggestions as to who might have strung that wire across his path, let alone why.

Longarm asked, "What's the story on that lawsuit your boss is handling for Duke Albright? Something about another boundary dispute with a homesteader called Dormouse?"

She smiled wanly and said, "Dorman, Silas Dorman, and I'm not at liberty to discuss a case that's under adjudication. That means—"

"I know how to say a case ain't been tried yet," he told her. "I get to spend a heap of time in courthouses, thanks to the way gents like your boss go on about picky bits of legal fluff. I hope a legal secretary as smart as you can see I'd doubtless be able to get the story from the other side, seeing they're the ones taking your client to law."

She shrugged, and primly declared she had no say in what the other side might or might not have to say to outsiders outside court. As she added he'd get nothing about it out of her, he decided Rathbone was getting his money's worth out of the pretty little thing. He had to admire an employee that loyal, even if she was employed by a son of a bitch he'd sure like to punch at least once.

He could see by the clock on one wall and the way the gal in charge kept hovering by that it was getting late. So he told them both he meant to come back as soon as he had more things to look up, and told the blonde, "I got to see a stage coach off in a few minutes, Miss Florence. But I'd be proud to escort you anywhere you have to go, seeing this is a cow town with the workday just about done."

She smiled incredulously, and assured him no cowboy with a lick of sense would pester a proper lady who worked for such an important law firm, whether she was escorted in public or not.

So he just ticked his hat brim to the both of them and headed out alone. Knowing where he was going, and not wanting either of the surviving killers to worry about it too soon, Longarm made his way by back streets to where that coach-and-six stood parked in a dusty lot before picking up more passengers for the night run to the south.

They had a young kid, likely from the neighborhood, sitting in the jehu's seat as if he was driving the six tethered mules as they enjoyed their own nose-bag suppers. The kid was there to make sure nobody really drove off while the crew and passengers were out of sight next door. The coach looked empty down below the kid's rump. It likely was, unless somebody else had worked around between the off side and that long blank wall to slither inside and lay low.

Longarm strolled along the far side of the lot, as if meaning to take a leak in the alley along its rear. The kid glanced his way, but seemed to lose interest in him as he just kept drifting along the far fence line. Then Longarm was in that alley, and as he risked a casual glance he saw that the kid's small head, barely visible above the top of the coach at this angle, was turned the other way.

Longarm moved along the alley until he was even with the long whitewashed wall the coach stood parked against. From where he now stood, in the dappled shade of a box elder in a weed-grown back corner of the lot, he could spot anyone out to enter that coach before its official stop at the hotel up the way. Unless they already had. That kid would know if some friendly cuss had come along to say he needed a ride south and meant to settle up with the crew about his fare as soon as they came back from supper in the tricky gloaming light.

But asking such a question from ground level could get a lawman shot before he heard a polite answer. So Longarm figured it might be safer to just ease along the wall and peek inside before he yelled questions at anybody. So that was what he was doing, and he'd made it two-thirds of the way to the baggage boot of the parked coach when a familiar voice yelled, "Custis! Down!" and somebody cut loose in the uncertain vicinity with a six-gun!

Longarm was on his belly, against the wall, with his Winchester aimed back the way he'd come, through a clump of tumbleweed, as Jeff Wade called, "Over here! I *got* the son of a bitch!"

Longarm spotted Jeff in the shade of that short but stocky box elder before he made out the crumpled denim mass at Wade's feet. Longarm got back to his own feet as the kid behind him started to yell like hell. The bemused lawman ignored that fuss. He knew what the kid was fussing about. He strode back to where his old pal was still holding a smoking six-gun on a total stranger sprawled in the dust and said, "You got him, all right. You don't have to bother with a pulse when that much of a man's skull's been blown away. What makes you so mean, Jeff?"

Wade replied as casually, "You can't see it without we roll him over, but he's laying atop the ivory-gripped Remington he was fixing to backshoot you with for some reason."

Longarm poked at the tooled leather gun rig across the dead man's denim-clad hips with the muzzle of his saddle gun. "I'd say his reasons were obvious. How come you were tailing him, Jeff?"

Jeff Wade smiled incredulously and replied, "Ain't that as obvious? I got eyes as good as yourn, and the Mex that used to wear that very gun rig was working for *me* when this back-shooting prick drygulched him! I spotted him coming out of the Venetian Garden Saloon not five minutes ago, and recognized Diego's hardware and harness on sight. I never let on I had, of course. I let him walk past me as bold as a rooster with no rivals on the dung heap, then followed him from half a pistol shot back to see where he was going. You want to guess where he was going, Custis?"

Longarm sighed and said, "I was hoping to head him off before he caught his ride out of town. Let's see if we can't take that third one alive."

Jeff Wade started to ask a dumb question. Then he nodded and said that third one riding the less distinctive army mount might not mean to board any stage, seeing he'd hung on to the horse.

Longarm got out his badge to pin it to the front of his own sun-faded trail duds as the stage crew and at least half the town seemed to be coming through the weeds of the lot toward them.

83

Jess suggested, "What if I round up some pals and we see if we can head that third jasper off, or cut his trail if he's left by now?"

Longarm grimaced and said, "A rider you don't know, aboard a mount nobody recalls, along a public thoroughfare, Jeff? You go along and ride in circles all night if you like. I'd as soon not tag along if it's all the same with you!"

Chapter 11

Doc Miller and the sheriff agreed things were getting mighty tedious in Elbert County, but this time Longarm got to dictate and sign a shorter statement. That kid atop the coach hadn't seen a thing before he'd turned to see it was all over, and naturally the Overland crew and passengers having supper next door had seen far less. So they told the kid to go on home, and let the coach leave after making dead certain nobody was aboard that Sheriff Otis didn't know to howdy.

Jeff Wade told Longarm they'd fixed up a room for him out at the home spread. But Longarm said he'd as soon stay in town and get an earlier start on the paperwork at the land office and county clerk's in the morning. Longarm hated trying to track a crook on paper. So that may have been why he was so good at it. He didn't waste as much time on the spelling and punctuation as a born file clerk might have, and hence caught only the names and numbers he found suspicious on the fly flipping pages. Knowing they'd never stand for him bringing anyone in who was wanted on a state or county charge, he'd eliminated a lot of minor federal charges right off. But of course it might be interesting to see just who might have strung a fence here or dug an irrigation ditch there on land nobody had ever discussed with the land office.

He took himself and his possibles over to that one hotel that was also the Overland stop. Since he was alone, and the night was still young, he was down in the tap room, enjoying a late snack of pickled pig's feet and needled beer, when Jeff Wade, Seth Mathis, and a half-dozen other older men stormed in as if they were mad as hell at him.

But it turned out they were expecting him to saddle up and go night riding with them. For some son of a bitch named Duke Albright had just thrown a firebrand into the hayloft out to the Dorman spread and two ponies had burned up along with the whole infernal barn!

Longarm whistled, and asked how come they'd told him about it before reporting it to their sheriff. Seth Mathis snorted in disgust and said, "Otis and his own deputies have already headed out to tisk and tush at the Dorman spread, as if Albright or his paid firebugs are likely to be hiding in Dorman's shit-house. We demanded he deputize us all and lead the damned way to Duke Albright's. But he said you can't posse up before you know who you're after."

Longarm washed down some pickled pork with his beer scuttle and soberly declared, "He's right. Did anybody see Albright or a known associate setting fire to Dorman's barn?"

Another local stockman snapped, "Nobody had to! Silas Dorman had Albright in court this very afternoon, and Lawyer Rathbone never would have bought that postponement if he and his client had had a leg to stand on!"

Jeff Wade nodded and said, "You were the one who said to start with the simple answers, that time we had trouble with stock thieves along the Goodnight-Loving Trail, remember?"

Longarm said, "I do. Simple is the best place to start. But you cut sign near the beginning of a trail, not at the address of some not-too-popular cuss who could have done it. Mike Otis was right to go on out to the scene of the crime and commence from there. As for how simple some answers may seem, I talked to Lawyer Rathbone just this afternoon, and he didn't strike me as stupid enough to set fire to the hayloft of the plaintiff he'd just stalled in court. Lawyers ask for such delays in the hopes the other side will cool off, wear down, and be willing to settle out of court. You don't hardly calm anyone down by torching their hay and killing their stock!"

Seth Mathis said, "You're talking as if Duke Albright had common sense or paid a lick of attention to his lawyer. We know Rathbone's tried to talk sense to his client. More than one of us has heard him. But Albright's one of them people who can't seem to see right from wrong. Old boys who were over to the courthouse today say they heard Duke Albright telling Silas Dorman to back off if he knew what was good for him. They heard old Silas sass the bully right back, and now the sun was barely down before Dorman's hay and ponies went up in smoke. So are you with us or not, Mister Long?"

Longarm smiled thinly and said, "I ain't a mister. I'm a federal deputy, sworn to uphold the law and defend the constitutional rights of everyone but 'Indians not Taxed.' So just what might you gents have in mind, once you all ride out to Albright's armed with all that righteous indignation?"

Jeff Wade said, "We mean to demand some answers, Custis."

Longarm raised a brow. "Answers to what? Are you expecting him to own up to attempted intimidation by means of arson in the first degree? This may come as a shock to you, Jeff. But I've had damned few night riders confess felonies to me just because I asked. Give Mike Otis time to gather some evidence before you ride off half cocked. I hope you all know that you'd be in peril of a compounded felony charge if you hurt anybody out yonder, even if they turned out to be guilty."

Another angry man protested, "Hold on! We got the right to protect our own lives and property, don't we?"

Longarm nodded soberly and said, "Duke Albright's life and property don't belong to you. You run him off or burn him out and you'll be doing just what you're accusing him of. You'll be interfering with due process of law by committing illegal acts of violence. That's what they call gunning suspects or burning 'em out without a trial, acts of violence."

Seth Mathis snapped, "Let's go, boys. We're wasting time arguing about the price of eggs when we could be out busting some."

There came a muffled roar of approval. Jeff Wade told Longarm in a gentler way, "They're going either way, Custis. Don't you want to help me steer them straight and narrow?"

Longarm shook his head. "Ain't you talking about that primrose path to perdition, pard? Old Marshal Vail would spank me good and make me eat my badge if I rode with half-ass vigilantes whilst vacationing with friends! Get 'em all to go on home, if you have any powers to steer 'em anywheres, Jeff. This ain't Californee in the Rush of '49. You're an easy ride from the capital of a state that don't hold with vigilance committees. So even if Mike Otis may be willing to forget and forgive a tad of night riding, you'll have the Colorado Guard on your asses if there's any bloodshed or serious property damage!"

Jeff sighed and said, "You're talking just like Sheriff Otis. I expected more from a pal I once saw demolishing a saloon after one of our drag riders got cheated."

Longarm smiled sheepishly and replied, "I run off to a war without asking permission one time too. I'm a grown-up peace officer these days, Jeff. You're supposed to be the adult head of a whole family as well. So don't you reckon it's time we both started to act our ages?"

Jeff said, "Seth's right. We're wasting time. We'll talk about our creaky knees and gray hairs later, Custis. Right now I got to go see another cuss about some childish actions!"

Longarm turned back to the bar and picked up a deviled egg from their free-lunch tray, late as they were serving it. It had watching an old pal make a total sap of himself beat by a mile.

Jeff hushed another man in the group who made a sneering remark about yellow streaks as they went out. It was some comfort to know Jeff wasn't really sore at him. Longarm knew how all of them felt. He'd just met Duke Albright and hadn't liked him even a bit. But this old world could wind up mighty empty if gents were allowed to do anything they wanted to anyone they didn't much like.

As he finished his beer and ordered another, Longarm reflected on how local bullies like Duke Albright got to be disliked just by treading on the toes of anyone they wanted to.

The barkeep was a good sport about a stranger dressed cow cleaning up the deviled eggs. Or maybe he didn't worry because it wasn't safe to keep deviled eggs overnight in weather as warm as they'd been having since that blizzard.

There weren't any fancy gals hanging around a hotel tap room at that hour, but somebody started the player piano against the rear wall, and things livened up a mite as gents drifted in for an after-supper drink or more with the boys.

Longarm was still surprised to see who two of the boys were. He had to nod at Duke Albright and Lawyer Rathbone as they bellied up to the bar beside him. Albright looked pouty. He barely nodded back. Lawyer Rathbone smiled as sincerely as a pimp offering to show a Harvey Gal how she could make some real money, and told Longarm, "We heard you'd gunned another total stranger down the street. That's partly why I suggested my client here stay at my place here in town tonight."

Longarm said, "Wasn't me doing the shooting. I was the one the rascal seemed anxious to backshoot. I don't suppose you heard of that fire out to the Dorman spread?"

Rathbone nodded. "That's what inspired us to appear in public some more like this. I don't know why, but it does seem that every time a bird shits on someone's hat my client here gets all the credit. If you're asking where Mister Albright was just after sundown, when they say that fire started to the dulcet tones of pounding hooves, I can produce plenty of witnesses to the fact we were enjoying a sit-down supper, with his palomino stabled out back with other witnesses."

Longarm growled, "I wasn't asking. I ain't in the habit of asking stupid questions. Did you ever hear how neither Major Murphy nor Jimmy Dolan of the Murphy-Dolan House in Lincoln County, New Mexico, were ever anywheres near when the more noisy events of that Lincoln County War were taking place?"

Rathbone went right on smiling as he purred, "Don't be so subtle. Come right out and make the charge if you think my client is masterminding some Machiavellian plot."

Longarm snorted, "There was nothing Machiavellian about that Lincoln County War. The mule-headed assholes on both sides went and ate each other up, like that gingham dog and calico cat in the kids' nursery rhyme. Tunstall and McSween on the one side and Murphy on the other wound up dead, along with numerous hired guns and a sheriff who should have been ashamed of his fool self for taking sides. Last I heard, Jimmy Dolan had run off flat broke. Henry McCarty, better known as Billy the Kid, is hiding out somewhere on the owlhoot trail with no more to show for all that fuss but a price on his young head. None of you assholes who go on about old Nick Machiavelli seem to savvy what he was trying to tell us. He wrote down all that sneaky shit the Borgias pulled as a warning, not a recommendation!"

Longarm wet his whistle with more beer and continued. "If you read old Nick out, instead of just skimming for the dirty tricks, you'll see he was against having sneaks like that mean prince running things. He was all for his poor shot-up Italy being a republic, more than two hundred years before we told that king of England the very same thing!"

Lawyer Rathbone dryly observed, "I assure you I've read the classics all the way through. Which of those dirty tricks in *Il Principe* are you charging my client with this evening?"

Longarm said, "If I had charges to make I'd make 'em. You're the one dancing a sarcastic minuet this evening. I was giving you and Duke here friendly advice. Starting neighborhood feuds for fun and profit can lead to not much fun and even less profit."

Duke Albright grabbed his smaller lawyer by one shoulder to move him out of the way as he stepped close enough to breathe his whiskey fumes in Longarm's face and bluster, "Are you trying to scare us, you big wind from Denver Town?"

Longarm resisted the natural impulse to move back just as far as a man needed to breathe in such rough company. He knew the bully wanted him to. He stood his ground and quietly said, "Get your fool nose out of my face before I bite it off. I ain't sure what I'm trying to convey to the likes of you. They're right about you, Duke. You're a dumb obnoxious asshole."

The bully of the county, almost as tall and far heavier than the lawman he couldn't seem to budge, said, "I ain't used to being called an asshole, mister."

Longarm lightly replied, "Do tell? I find it hard to believe not a single soul has ever told you the simple truth before. How come you act like such an asshole if you don't want to be known as an asshole, Asshole?"

Duke Albright went for his tied-down Colt '74. He froze with his big fist on the grips as he found himself staring down the barrel of a .44-40 and heard Longarm calmly asking,

"Want to see me do it again? I generally give one free demonstration when I find myself in the company of an asshole with a big mouth and a slow draw. I don't give second chances. It's been my experience that when a man draws on me after I've told him not to do that no more, he really means to kill or be killed."

Lawyer Rathbone pleaded, "Cut it out! Both of you! I never took you out for a drink to get you killed, Duke!"

Albright neither drew nor removed his hand from the grips of his own gun as he sullenly asked, "Ain't you taking a lot for granted, Nat? Who's to say who might or might not die around here if this Denver boy don't watch his damn step!"

Rathbone groaned, "Me! You're going up against the fastest gun in Colorado and he's got the drop on you, Duke!"

Albright said, "Aw, he ain't all that much. I don't see horns and a tail. Do you?"

Longarm knew what Albright was doing. It was astounding to meet a grown man, sober enough to stand up, playing such kid games. But Longarm had never liked them when he'd had them played on him out in the schoolyard long ago and far away. So knowing how many other local kids were watching to see how their schoolyard bully might make out, Longarm quietly put his six-gun back in its holster and moved clear from the bar, quietly saying, "Ready when you are, Asshole."

That wasn't the way the game was supposed to be played in Duke Albright's schoolyard. Feeling that nobody expected more of a man when somebody had the drop on him, Albright had thought it was safe to sound defiant, staring down at a gun he knew wasn't about to go off. But things suddenly took on a whole new tingle as Longarm purred, "My double-action side arm can get off its first round a fraction of a second sooner than that thumb-buster you're packing. After that the advantage shifts your way. I'm stuck with cross-draw whilst you've already got your hand on your tied-down side-draw gun. So why ain't you drawing it, Asshole?"

Lawyer Rathbone protested, "This is cold-blooded murder in front of witnesses!"

To which Longarm quietly replied, "No, it ain't. Your client, the asshole, was first to go for his gun. I'm still waiting to see if he means it or not. If he does, I got the right to defend myself. If he don't, I suggest you take him home and put him to bed. For you know how cranky some kids get when they stay up too late, not knowing just what in the hell they really want to do."

Albright almost whimpered, "Damn it, is he bluffing or ain't he? I can't tell, Nat!"

Rathbone said quietly, "He's not bluffing, and even if you won, I don't know how I'd ever get you off. Let's go, Duke. I read that book by Machiavelli too. He writes it's a smart general who knows when to advance and when to retreat, and this is certainly not the time to push it one inch further!"

So they left, the lawyer soothing and Duke Albright fixing to either bust out crying or bite somebody's head off. With his sort of cuss it was hard to tell.

As they vanished from sight, an older man who'd been sitting a bit tensely by the piano rose to tell the barkeep, "This Denver boy is fixing to have another on me, Larry. For I've been out this way many a year, and this is the first time I've ever seen anyone act so astonishing, outside the pages of one of Beadle's dime novels, I mean!"

The barkeep took Longarm's scuttle to put a head on it as he replied with a grin, "Duke Albright's been acting like one of them Wild West badmen ever since he blew into these parts, and it's about time someone took him up on it!"

Then the barkeep sighed and said, "It's too bad Duke backed down like that. Think of all the trouble it might save the rest of us if this young gent had shot it out with the ugly mutt!"

Chapter 12

Longarm was coming out of the county clerk's the next morning when he met up with Sheriff Otis. The sheriff got right down to brass tacks by saying, "I missed out on all the fun you and your pal, Jeff Wade, were having last night. Just heard about the way you ran Duke Albright out of that tap room."

Longarm smiled sheepishly and replied, "Somebody had to leave. I'd already paid for my room there. I wasn't showing off. I was proving what I'd already suspected. Duke Albright is mean, but he ain't crazy-mean. I figured he'd back down if I growled just as much."

Longarm reached casually for a couple of cheroots as he added that he hadn't seen old Jeff and the boys of late.

The sheriff accepted the offered smoke and even let Longarm light him up, but said, "If you catch up with him first, tell Jeff Wade I'd like a word with him about his manners. I don't hold with vigilance committees, seeing the voters of this county elected me to maintain the damned peace and quiet in these parts!"

Longarm lit his own cheroot and mildly replied, "I suggested much the same thing last night, Sheriff. You say somebody busted the law outright?"

Otis grumbled, "That's what I want to talk to Jeff about. Lucky for all concerned, Duke Albright was in town, getting rawhided by *you*, when Jeff and his night riders showed up out to his home spread. Some of the boys wanted to drive off some stock and set some hay to blazing just the same. Fortunately, Jeff and some of the other more responsible children kept them in line, saying their beef was with Albright, not his hired help. But it was still way the hell closer than us elected county officials can abide, and it best not happen again!"

Longarm nodded, and said he'd pass the suggestion on to Jeff if he met up with him first. The somewhat mollified sheriff asked him what he'd been looking for in the county clerk's.

Longarm sighed and said, "Some pattern that makes even a lick of sense. Since all us grown-ups agree Duke Albright is bluffing more than he let's on, and has the wherewithal to boss around a sizeable herd of livestock and lawyers, there ought to be some method in his madness."

He waved his lit cheroot at the door he'd just come out of as he added, "I was looking to cut a paper trail in your county files. As a general rule the self-appointed bully of the town is slicing himself more pie than he really deserves. You ruin your neighbors in order to buy 'em out cheap. No grown man stomps on toes for no good reasons."

Sheriff Otis suggested, "Mayhaps Duke Albright ain't a grown man. I've tried in vain to backtrack him to where he might have learned to act so ornery and get so rich."

Longarm nodded. "I wasn't able to find anything on file to indicate where the jackass came from either. Could you tell me who Quinn, Baker, or Heinz, all Esquires, might be? I kept tripping over those three names on property deeds, but not one appears on your roll of voting freeholders inside."

Otis made a wry face and explained, "That's 'cause the

three of 'em vote elsewheres. Quinn and Baker are a law firm down Pueblo way. Lawyer Heinz practices over in Denver. Nat Rathbone represents them here in Elbert County. They do as much for him when he gets sued in their courts. All four of 'em seem to get sued a heap."

Longarm said, "So I noticed. They sure string fences and dam up branchwaters a country mile or more from any property they hold any title to. Can any man file a homestead claim in one county and run a law firm in another, Sheriff?"

Otis shrugged and said, "You'd have to ask at the federal land office. But don't some British beef firms own good-sized cow spreads out our way?"

Longarm frowned thoughtfully and replied, "Wasn't talking about an absentee landlord owning land he'd bought and paid for. Those pals of Lawyer Rathbone and Duke Albright are listed as owners or part owners of homestead claims, proven or unproven, and I reckon I *will* ask the land office to explain how that can be allowable."

They shook on it and parted friendly. Longarm would have gone directly to the land office from there if that library hadn't been open along the way.

He went inside to find that same mousy little brown-headed gal alone at her counter. He introduced himself more formally, having more time to spare this time. But when he told her what sort of books he wanted to borrow and read later up in his hotel room, she looked as if he'd asked for a kiss and protested, "Oh, no, I couldn't lend out books to anyone who didn't have one of our library cards!"

He tried to be a good sport, lest he make such a shy but stubborn county official cry. He said he'd be proud to apply for a card right then and there, adding, "I'm paid up to the end of the week over at the Overland Hotel. So I'd say that makes me a legal resident of Kiowa Township as well as Elbert County, wouldn't you?"

She said she didn't know, and so he'd have to fill out a form and wait until she had the approval of her superior, the boss librarian, who never showed up before noon. The inferior librarian he was stuck with added her boss, Miss Hamilton, was a "dear" about showing up in time for her to take a whole hour off for noon dinner.

Longarm allowed he was pleased to hear nobody was allowed to starve on the premises, but insisted, "It ain't as if I just asked to borrow a book of poetry or even *Twenty Thousand Leagues under the Sea* for a porch-swing read to while away my stay in Kiowa."

Then he thought and quickly added, "Before we have us a duel at fifteen paces over that library card, ma'am, let's determine what you have on hand to fight over. What I'm looking for is one or more of those local history tomes you usually find in the library at a county seat. I know this county's spanking new. But it often seems some old-timer who's been there six months to a year longer than a heap of Johnny-come-latelies seems to have the local history and a grove of the older family trees printed up at his own expense."

The mousy but not downright homely librarian nodded gravely and said, "I know exactly what you mean, and as a matter of fact several of our founding families have had such limited editions printed up by a Denver firm. The recorded history of the Ballard family would be the one you'd want to read for local history as well as gossip. Fred Ballard Senior and his four grown sons claimed homesteads here in Elbert County during the war, when Roman Nose and his Cheyenne Crooked Lancers made that a mighty risky way to come by short-grass prairie!"

Longarm nodded soberly and said that was the sort of local color he was interested in. She told him to come back later that afternoon.

He managed not to swear. It wasn't easy. He explained,

again, he was a lawman investigating their fool county for them on his own vacation time, and added he had to get on back to Denver in the near future.

She dimpled sweetly but stubbornly, and said she'd take down his application and then deliver his card and the four books he'd likely find most useful to his hotel, once Miss Hamilton said she could.

He doubted he was apt to get a better offer from such a small young thing. So he took her infernal paper forms over to a reading table and filled them out.

Once he had, she showed him through the stacks in the back, and even took down the expensively bound books she'd said he might find most illuminating.

She said she'd keep the four of them under her counter for him until such time as her boss said he could borrow them. She tried to cheer him up, or keep him around for company, by adding it would be all right with her if he wanted to go through one or more of them at the reading table, as long as he didn't leave the building with any.

He shook his head with a smile, and allowed he had other stuff to read at the nearby land office. She looked sort of wistful once she saw she'd have all those damned dusty books to herself for a spell.

Longarm ambled on to the smaller land office. He found it far more crowded. That same older gal was there, as expected, along with that same ash-blonde who worked for Lawyer Rathbone. But better yet, the federal county agent in charge was also there, a stocky cuss who reminded Longarm a tad of his own boss back in Denver, the somewhat older and balder Marshal Billy Vail.

The county agent answered to the handle of Prescott, and said he was proud to shake with the famous Longarm. "Heard about the way you crawfished Duke Albright last night. About time somebody took the measure of that blowhard!"

Longarm didn't look at Florence Redfern, knowing any expression she saw on his face could be read any way a gal whose loyalties lay with a client wanted to read it. Aware that anything he said was surely going back to Lawyer Rathbone, and Duke Albright, he shrugged and asked, "Have you ever noticed how a spilled coffee can get to be a raging flood of molten lava by the time it's been discussed half-a-dozen times? I never came to brag about a tap-room tiff. I came in the hopes a man who rides herd on federal homestead claims might know more than me about the rules and regulations."

Prescott modestly agreed they paid him to worry about such local federal matters. "To the extent any man born of mortal woman has ever understood government claims and counter-claims, that is. The jaspers we elect in our infinite wisdom keep making up new rules without bothering to read the old ones, and sometimes we wind up with Kansas trains."

Longarm laughed. Most everyone who dealt with the law west of the Mississippi knew about the railroad regulation passed by the Kansas Legislature in what should have been a sober moment, considering the way Kansas felt about hard liquor.

It was still the dead-serious law of Kansas that whenever a train running one way met a train running the other way, whether on one or two tracks, both trains were required to come to a complete stop and neither was to move forward or backward until the other passed it.

Before Longarm could ask about other fool laws, the ash-blonde at the nearby reading table sweetly piped up to ask Longarm if his "Mexican spitfire" had caught up with him yet.

Longarm looked sincerely confused, and allowed he hadn't known he owned a Mexican of any description. The older gal who worked there said, as her boss nodded, that a Señorita Cortez had just been in there asking about him within the hour.

Prescott said, "She seemed anxious to find you. Said something about the sheriff telling her you might be here."

Longarm frowned thoughtfully. "Makes sense if her name's really Capaz instead of Cortez. They wired his kin down Publo way about Diego Capaz getting drygulched yesterday. Somebody named Capaz would naturally come up this way to claim the poor kid's cadaver. But I hope they don't expect *me* to tell 'em what happened to old Diego. Sheriff Otis knows as much as me. You say she already talked to him?"

The ash-blonde dryly observed, "I'm sure the sheriff assured her you were the lawman who accounted for one of her late kinsman's killers yesterday. She said she had something to tell you. I've no idea why she keeps insisting on calling you a bragging lardo."

Longarm felt it might be bragging if he explained Brazo Largo was the Spanish for Arm Long. They said lots of things backward in Spanish.

He asked instead, "How come you called her a spitfire? Might the poor gal have seemed upset?"

The two land office folks nodded. Flo Redfern wrinkled her pert nose and asked what he'd call a fandango dancer of twenty-odd summers who batted her eyelashes at men like clicking castanets.

Agent Prescott's jowls got a shade pinker as he protested the poor little Mexican gal was doubtless anxious to seem friendly in a strange Anglo town.

The more motherly clerical gal smiled sort of knowingly as she nodded and seemed to agree with the both of them. Longarm said he'd find out later if the Capaz gal from Puelbo was a fandango dancer or just unsure of herself. He turned back to Prescott and, seeing there was no way of doing it behind that law clerk's back, asked the county agent straight out if you were allowed to file a homestead claim in one county and meanwhile do business and reside in another.

Prescott nodded soberly. "I know who you're talking about. All fourteen of them. The answer to your question is no and yes. The Homestead Act of '62 was designed to fill the West with white folks, not paragons of virtue, or even citizens who could read and write. Since a homesteader can hardly be expected to make a living off land he's been confined to as a prisoner, a claim-holder is naturally allowed to be on or off his claim at a given moment."

"Long enough to reside and *vote* in other parts?" Longarm demanded.

Prescott said, "I've heard a claim can be disallowed if nobody has made any improvements after five years or if it can be shown he or she has left the land unoccupied for more than six months out of any one year. Before you ask the obvious, somebody would have to file on the same land or make a formal complaint against the accused claim-holder. We simply don't have the manpower to ride around making sure some homesteader really means to come home from his shopping in town, a cattle drive, or whatever."

Longarm said, "I'll buy that, if you can tell me how one jasper's handle can appear on more than one claim or title deed."

Prescott could. It sounded tedious, but it boiled down to anyone grubstaking the official claim-holder for a less-than-fifty-percent share in the enterprise. When Longarm named some names, in spite of the ash-blonde sitting there with her ear cocked, Prescott said those lawyers, along with other businessmen, acted as junior partners in some cases and outright owners in others. Once a claim was proven, it became a quarter section of Colorado real estate to be bought and sold like any other.

Longarm nodded. "In sum, these mighty generous backers have been grubstaking fly-by-night homesteaders who tend to sell out their fifty-odd percentages and just ride off into the sunset. It's not the way *I'd* give public lands away, no offense, but let's talk about the way land still mapped as purely public open range seems to be getting fenced, ditched, and in sum total *hogged* by the likes of Duke Albright and the pals he has fronting for him in these parts."

Prescott sighed and said, "I wish we didn't have to talk about Land Management's conflicting open-range regulations. They want us to enforce them. How would you resolve that regulation about railroading in Kansas without looking the other way a lot?"

Longarm said, "I was told before I got here that wire had been strung across open range to keep stock away from water it's grown up on. On my way in I had to cut two fences strung smack across a federal post road and public right-of-way. I reckon you've heard of that fence and irrigation ditch on open range cutting Silas Dorman off from the road to town or market?"

At the nearby table, Flo Redfern piped up. "That's exactly what I've been going through these land office files to resolve, Deputy Long. Silas Dorman has brought suit against our client on the basis of a needed improvement blocking an access road the Dormans laid out across open range with no more authority."

"Way earlier," Prescott objected, adding with a weary sigh, "I told you it was tedious to get into. Secretary of the Interior Carl Schurz just ordered a full investigation of such abuses, with a view to uniform federal range laws. You're hardly the first person who's ever noticed we could *use* some. But as of here and now, there simply aren't that many fair or even sensible laws on the books. How did you think the law firm this young lady works for manages to get so many postponements over to the courthouse? Dorman's lawyer has been in here going through the same files. I told him what I've told Miss

Redfern here. Trying a case involving so many conflicting state and federal statutes would be beyond the wisdom of Solomon and the patience of Job!"

Flo Redfern announced rather smugly, "Call me Sheba and tell me what's so complicated about this nuisance suit. I've found any number of ways the Dormans can get from their quarter section to here or most anywhere, provided they simply drive across a little undisputed open range!"

Longarm had looked over the Dorman legal brief at the county clerk's. So he said, "Takes longer to drive a dozen miles than it does two furlongs, Miss Sheba. I won't ask anybody working for any lawyer to concern themselves with what sound fair. But how can you just shut down an established wagon trace across open range you have no more right to your ownself?"

The shapely, pretty, but hard-looking gal answered simply, "You just shut it down, the way they shut down Shawnee Trail, the Chisholm Trail, and just recently, the Santa Fe Trail. You tell people to use the Ogallala or to sue you, if they must, because you have much more important improvements to make and grazing or rights-of-passage rank lower by far in the winning of this Great American Desert."

Longarm shot a questioning smile at Prescott, who shrugged and replied, "I said Secretary Schurz was working on it. As of now, I fear she's right. There's nothing on the books to stop anyone from using and abusing open range most any fool way, and as you may have noticed, possession and court delays is nine-tenths of the way they play their game!"

Longarm nodded thoughtfully and quietly asked, "Then what's the game we're playing in these parts? I've rid high and I've rid low in peace and war across these High Plains, and I'll be switched with live snakes if I can make anything but kid stuff by a schoolyard bully out of anything I've seen since I first started looking!"

The ash-blonde demurely assured him her boss and his client were honest and upright, as the court would surely prove if ever old Silas Dorman got Albright into court.

Longarm said, "I don't mean to hold my breath, Miss Sheba. Could I be the first one in these parts to guess at the next move once you just can't put the case off another six or eight months?"

She just smiled innocently. But since Prescott and the lady who clerked for him looked curious, Longarm said, "Dorman brought suit against Duke Albright because it was a work crew off his spread who fenced off Dorman's wagon trace and dug that fool irrigation ditch across it. But neither Duke nor none of his provable business pards has a freehold or homestead claim at either end of that so-called improvement, which is nothing more than a half mile of fence and a long dry hole in the ground. There might be some water in such a grand irrigation channel right after a rain. But the rest of the time it runs from a furlong north of Dorman's wagon trace to another furlong south, serving no purpose on earth save to cut Silas Dorman off from the post road."

Flo Redfern nodded and volunteered, "Mister Dorman could simply drive around the improvement our client has begun with a view to future development along that post road, as I just said."

It was Prescott, knowing the range he was supposed to manage, who whistled thoughtfully and said, "Now that's mighty raw, even for a range hog like Duke Albright."

He saw his clerk didn't understand what they were jawing about, and explained, "Duke's so-called irrigation project runs from one deep brushy gully to another, leaving the Dorman claim cut off on the higher flat stretch between."

Flo Redfern still insisted, "They can drive a few miles east, to where those little erosion channels peter out on wider open range."

Prescott muttered, "Sure they can. Meanwhile Duke Albright's sure to settle the long-drawn-out case by simply buying Silas Dorman out."

The county agent turned to Longarm to grumble, "He's done that a time or more before. Bought the Brandons out a couple of years ago for less than they'd spent proving their claim and getting a clear title to sell."

"How come?" asked Longarm with a puzzled smile.

Prescott said, "The Brandons went broke on improvements they thought they were going to pay for with garden truck to market in Denver. What the grasshoppers left was too nibbled and stained with grasshopper spit for those fancy housewives in the city. They say Ed Brandon got next to nothing for the barley he finally managed to truck into a Denver brewery. We all *told* him this was livestock country. But you know what they say about a fool and his money. So when Duke Albright was the only one who offered, Brandon had to sell at Albright's price."

Longarm shook his head and said, "That ain't what I asked. I know why two out of three homestead claims fail to pan out. What I find a real poser is how come Albright paid a thing for the place. I was out there just yesterday with Skinny Pryor scouting for sign. I saw little more than fence poles and rusted-out bob around a quarter section of short-grass, some ruined sod construction, and nary a neighbor for a serious ride in all directions."

Before the county agent could answer, Flo Redfern got up from her place at the reading table as if she'd just been scared by a spider like Miss Muffet. But she managed to look calm enough as she declared it was almost noon and so she had to get back to her office before old Nathan Rathbone, Esquire, lit out for some business dinner.

As she almost ran out the front door, Longarm soberly asked the two land office folks, "Have you ever had the feeling somebody was afraid you were about to ask a question before you could get around to answering it?"

Prescott looked blank at first, suddenly brightened, and snapped his fingers, saying, "By gum, she must have worked on that title search and property transfer, her boss being Albright's lawyer!"

The motherly gal who backed Prescott's play still seemed confused as she demanded, "What do I seem to be missing here? I remember how the Brandons sold out and moved on after putting in those five years of hard work out there on that lonesome prairie. But what's all the fuss about a richer landholder snapping up their proven claim for next to nothing?"

Longarm explained, "Next to nothing is still something, and that abandoned homestead is miles from any of Albright's other holdings. Which is doubtless why he's been maintaining it so well."

Turning back to Prescott, he asked if they had a smaller-scale land plat showing the good-sized county as a whole.

They did, and since they were both commencing to follow his drift, the old gal was the one who hauled it out of a file drawer to spread across the table Flo Redfern had left to them.

Prescott allowed light pencil marks wouldn't do any permanent damage as he proved he earned his keep as the county agent. He was able to indicate all the quarter sections Albright owned outright with little A's. It helped a lot that the chart had already been marked off for homestead claims, past and future, by the BLM surveyors at the time the land had first been thrown open to settlement.

The small A's formed a wide-scattered buckshot pattern, most but not all west of Kiowa Creek. Even the clerical gal could see there wasn't much of a pattern to see. Longarm asked about both the claims and purchases made by known kith or kin of the big range hog who seemed to be taking small scattered bites.

Prescott and his helper had to rustle up some papers to manage that chore. Longarm suggested they mark land held by known associates with the letter K, and just put a question mark where gossip had it that Albright had been behind the deal.

After they'd been doing that a spell, Prescott declared, "I see how they *might* wind up in position to make it tough to drive stock in to the Denver yards, given way more claims and a whole lot of ad hoc drift fencing betwixt one solid claim and another."

Longarm had already considered that. He asked, "Ain't it true, as confusing as our current range regulations might be, that a stockman driving to market has the right to flatten wire strung across his right-of-way across public federal range?"

"If he feels tough enough," Prescott replied, running his pencil tip along that post road Longarm had already found blocked as he continued. "There's no way even Duke Albright could hope to get away with shutting down this federal right-of-way long enough to affect the price of beef. But as you can see, this milky way of fenced-in quarter sections Albright and his pals seem to be amassing would not only complicate the roundups we've been holding in these parts, but make it nigh impossible to drive single or consolidated herds this more usual way, catty-corner over to Box Elder and northwest into Denver."

Longarm stared down at the emerging pattern for a spell before he decided, "Simpler on paper than out on the real range. Them few fractions of an inch on this chart add up to country miles of wide-open short-grass it'd take many a reel of Glidden wire and an army of fence riders to police."

He stabbed a finger down between two small squares marked with question marks. "Here's about as close a fit as Albright and his whole bunch may have managed. I still make it out to be at least a six-mile gap. That would mean a landowner out in the yard of this westernmost spread couldn't even see his neighbor to the east, and might not notice a thousand head of beef busting through any wire the two had strung betwixt 'em."

The old land office gal, who doubtless didn't ride the range so often, marveled that those particular plots looked closer than he'd just suggested.

Longarm nodded soberly and said, "Them best-laid plans that old Scotch poet mentioned have often been laid out on paper, ma'am. A heap of battles have been lost because some general read his maps a mite different from the way some troop leader in the field read the country he was riding through to the sounds of real guns."

Prescott nodded soberly down at the same grand design as he said, "I'm no stockman. But I know that rolling prairie betwixt here and the Denver yards too well to think I could control any large part of it with ten times as many pinprick quarter sections. So mayhaps our mysterious Duke Albright isn't really as experienced a range rider as he'd have us all believe?"

Longarm didn't want to say "asshole" in front of a lady. So he just shrugged and said, "Somebody seems to be missing something here. I sure hope it ain't me. It makes little or no sense for old Albright to keep snapping up small holdings, whether he encourages folks to sell out or not."

The motherly gal asked if it wasn't possible the Albright boy was simply just a big mean bully.

Longarm grimaced and replied, "Makes as much sense as anything else I can come up with, ma'am."

Chapter 13

Longarm was enjoying a porterhouse steak smothered in chili con carne at his hotel when that mousy little library gal came into the dining room with his neatly inscribed library card and those four books neatly wrapped in brown paper, as if they'd been printed in Paris, France, to sell to Americans.

Longarm rose from his own bentwood chair, and waved her down to another as he set her gifts to one side and asked if she'd rather have him order for her or do it herself. She looked nervously all about, and confided she wasn't used to ordering in such fancy dining establishments. That was what she called a seedy tin-ceiling bean hall in a third-rate transient hotel, a dining establishment. So he wasn't too surprised, once he'd called the waitress over and suggested the lady might go for their stuffed trout, mashed spuds, and fresh greens, to learn she was a little country, although a grammar school graduate off fifty acres of Ohio bottomland her daddy had owned outright. It was none of his beeswax what she was doing out on the High Plains with a wedding band on her right hand widow-woman style, so he didn't ask her.

She asked him how much such fancy grub was likely to cost her as they waited for the waitress to bring it out to her.

Longarm assured her the least he could offer a lady who'd gone to so much trouble was a free meal. She still protested, until he explained he was allowed to charge meals in the field to the taxpayers. That wasn't completely true, since he was in Kiowa on his own time, and it wouldn't have been fair to the taxpayers if he hadn't been, since she was neither a prisoner nor a material witness in his care. But it seemed to make her feel better. He'd noticed in the past how even taxpayers seemed to feel it was only right to stick the taxpayers for federal handouts.

He naturally slowed down, chewing thoroughly as he'd been told to as a boy, to give her the chance to catch up. He noticed that once she had, she ate fast, as if they'd been having a race to go on to their desserts. He resisted the impulse to warn her about fish bones as she shoveled her grub as if she hadn't eaten in days.

By the time they were ready to order dessert, less than ten minutes later, he'd learned her name was Cora and that she'd told her boss lady, the indulgent Miss Hamilton, she had a bit of shopping to do and might need as much as an hour and a half of the mid-day off.

Longarm had no idea why that ought to matter to him. He was just as glad she ate so quickly. He wanted to go through those books on the local history during the dinner-hour lull, when it might not matter as much whether he found anything calling for more questioning of the local populace. He was starting to worry about that. Nobody he'd been able to talk to so far had made a whole lot of sense.

Cora went along with his suggestion they have coffee with molasses pie for dessert. As they waited for it, he felt it might be rude to mention those bodies on display over to the funeral home, but told her he'd heard some kinswoman of Diego Capaz had been looking for him, and asked if the Mexican lady had by any chance tried the library.

Cora hesitated, then sounded sort of pouty as she nodded and told him, "I'd hardly call her a *lady*. Looked more like a woman of the town, if the town was Vera Cruz. We weren't sure you were the lawman the greasy thing was really after. She only said she wanted to ask somebody called Mister Largo something about her Herman. We told her the only lawman who'd been in all day was long gone. So she left, a tad flouncy, and it's just not warm enough, indoors or out, for any proper gal to flounce about in skirts cut that way with her ankles showing and her bodice exposing so much of her . . . throat."

Longarm washed down some of his sticky-sweet dessert—they'd made it with too much molasses—and asked if that other lady might not have been talking about her *hermano* instead of some gent called Herman.

Cora nodded. "She did put an O on the end of Herman, the way they will with their fancy airs."

Longarm explained, "*Hermano* means the same as brother in Spanish. I'd heard some of the dead boy's kin were up this way from Pueblo. I wish it was somebody more distant than a sister. I just hate to talk to ladies about dead husbands, brothers, and such when I don't have a sensible thing to add to what they already know."

Cora thought as she bolted down her own pie, then nodded as if she'd agreed with herself and said, "I do think she wanted to tell this Mister Largo something, once he told her more about what happened to her Herman. I don't know where she went from the library. She'd said she was in a hurry."

Longarm thought, then nodded, and said, "I'll ask over at that funeral parlor later. They ought to know where she'd be staying in town as they arrange to ship old Diego home, plant him here, or whatever."

He washed down the last bit of pie he cared to have and added, "Not much sense in looking for her right now. Whether she lives by our customs or her own, she'll be having her own dinner about now, and likely planning on at least a wash-up indoors with the noonday sun so hot today."

Cora said she'd heard about those Mexican siestas lasting all afternoon, and marveled that they ever got a thing done having such lazy ways.

Longarm gently explained, "La Siesta don't last all afternoon. Just through the hotter part of the day from, say, noon to three or four. It sounds lazier than it really is. Living mostly in sunny climates, the Latin breeds of folks keep different hours, not shorter hours. A shop shut down from noon to four might stay open past midnight if business is good. Mexican folks are regular night owls next to our own. There's a heap to be said for splitting your day up the way they do living in such climes. It takes a few days to get used to it south of the border, but once you do, it's surprising how much a body can get done, rising early and going to bed late with La Siesta in the middle."

She demanded, "You mean those greasy things don't really sleep as much as *we* do, Custis?"

He said, "I reckon they get the same eight hours or so, albeit busted up into four hours or so at a time. As to how greasy they may be, some wash regular while others don't, the same as us. That darker complexion some of 'em have is more often Indian blood. You say this Señorita Capaz seems sort of dusky?"

"Sort of Apache, now that you mention Indian blood!" the mousy brown-haired Ohio gal decided. Longarm was commencing to wish she'd go back to work. That Mexican gal sounded far more interesting, both to look at and to talk to.

Almost as if she'd read Longarm's mind, Cora gaped up at a clock on the dining room wall. "Heavens, we've been sitting here a good twenty minutes, as if we were rich swells who never had to get back to work. Did you say you were taking those books up to your own private room in this grand hotel?"

He started to say it wasn't so grand next to, say, the Tremont House or Palace in Denver. Then he decided not to low-rate what a somewhat more country gal considered grand surroundings. Knowing she'd doubtless brag about the swell twenty minutes she'd spent in a real hotel dining room, he just nodded gravely and assured her he had cross-ventilation and a steel-sprung bedstead of polished brass up on the top floor.

He hadn't expected her to ask if she could see it. Once she had, he saw no way short of being downright rude a man could refuse her. He wasn't sure many men would want to as they went out to the stairs and he let her go up them first. Her waspy waist and small round bottom were more evident from behind as she proceeded up ahead of him, bent over a tad. But of course, almost as soon as you had such thoughts about mousy library gals on their noon break, it was time to set such thoughts aside. So it was Cora, not him, who asked as she paused for breath on the landing if those Mexicans having siestas got all the way undressed for bed or just flopped down somewhere as they waited for the day to cool off.

He said, "I keep telling other Anglo folks our neighbors to the south come in as many shapes and sizes. But judging from some few I've known better, La Siesta usually adds up to a light meal and a lie-down dressed or undressed for the occasion."

As they started up again Cora coyly asked, over one shoulder, if he meant they undressed for bed thinking of the temperature or of such company as they might be keeping at the moment.

He quietly told her both might be considerations as he silently warned his fool crotch not to tingle that way. For she'd just *said* she had to get back to that library, in less than an hour as of now, and any man who hadn't been teased worse than this by more tempting teasers simply hadn't been around that many women.

Driving men to distraction, or at least to looking foolish, was just part of a woman's nature, bless their fickle twitchy hearts, and despite what some green hands at the game might think, it was the less-head-turning belles who went sort of loco themselves on the rare occasions they saw the chance to get the boys to walk picket fences for them.

So Longarm stayed cool and collected as he unlocked his corner room and offered the country gal a grand tour of his hired quarters. He was pleased to see the chambermaid had changed the bedding and hung fresh towels by the corner washstand. With the windows open and a fair breeze blowing in off the prairie, you couldn't smell that bug spray that had bothered him the night before, and he'd already made certain there were no bedbugs.

Cora sat on the edge of the bed, marveling as she made the springs bounce under her small shapely derriere. She dimpled roguishly up at him as he put the books on the wardrobe. He knew better than to grin back like an eager hound following a bitch in heat down an alley. Because that was when they got to say all men were alike, and a man had no way to defend his fool self when he was drooling.

But fair was fair, and when the no-longer-mousy snip said it hardly seemed worth undressing for a siesta lasting less than one hour, he took off his hat, removed his gun rig, and soberly assured her, "I can get you out of that summer frock and dressed again in no more than two full minutes either way, if that's what you're asking, Miss Cora."

She stared owlishly up at him, her mouth a little puckered rose bud as he calmly added, "If you'd rather we remained no more than friends, just say so and I'll see you back down to the lobby. You're a desirable woman and, being a man, I desire you, if that's what we desire to establish here. But having done

114

so, it's needless cruelty to dumb animals to make any more suggestions about getting undressed when we all know how unlikely such a miracle might be, Miss Cora."

She suddenly laughed like a mean little kid and declared, "You do have a romantic way with words, Custis. You really wouldn't try to stop me if I just thanked you for a lovely dinner and went back to work, would you?"

To which he could only reply, "Nothing else a proper gent could do, the lady having the final say in such matters."

She hesitated, reached up as if about to unpin her light brown hair, and calmly asked, "What would you do if I told you I might be able to excuse a two-hour shopping expedition and got some of this confining gingham out of the way, Custis?"

He knew better than to let her see how much he wanted her to do that, knowing how much it hurt when you stumbled this late in their game. He just moved over to shoot the bolt on the one door out to the hallway as he softly suggested she was welcome to stay as long as she cared to.

So naturally, her hair was down and her skirts were up as he turned back from the door, and seeing she was having a time getting the summer frock off, he moved to help her, and she went to work on his fly buttons as he slipped the calico up over her head. So seeing she was wearing nothing under her frock, doubtless because it was such an unseasonably warm day, and seeing it was already hard as she hauled it out of his jeans to marvel at, a good time was had by all as he simply fell across the bed with her and thrust home into her stark naked flesh while she enjoyed the novelty, she said, of all that fully clad passion on top of her.

But they both agreed it was even grander, a few minutes later, as they both went at it hammer and tongs without a stitch on either of them. He never asked where such a mousy little

115

thing had learned to bump and grind her finely proportioned little naked form so swell.

She didn't seem to care where he'd learned to position a lady atop two pillows and hit bottom without really hurting her either. There was much to be said for not having much time for such a good time. He never learned just how she'd gotten to be a widow woman out West, and he doubted she gave a hoot about that gal back home in West-by-God-Virginia who'd taught a neighborhood kid about doing it dog-style, seeing they'd already done it lots of other ways.

They made the next forty-odd minutes feel like a honeymoon, and then the next thing he knew he was lighting them a smoke as the breeze from the window cooled their lust-fevered flesh and Cora commenced to cry, bless her foolish nature.

He took a drag on his cheroot and held her closer in an understanding way, soothing her. "Nothing to get upset about, Miss Cora. I still think as highly of you, and what we just done was only human nature."

She sobbed, "I'm not upset because you just screwed me silly. I'm crying because it's over and I want some more!"

Before he could say anything a man might regret, she explained she couldn't come back once she returned to her boarding house, lest the other gals she roomed with suspect something. When she said she thought it might be best if they just quit while they were ahead, it made him feel so good he kissed her. Then, being they were both only human, they said good-bye right, and wound up on the rug as they were fixing to come again, with her on top and vowing to drag him on home with her and to hell with her mousy rep. It felt so good he said he'd be proud to spend the night with her and all those other gals at her boarding house.

But as that cynical old Frenchman had observed, the human mind was never more rational than right after a warm meal and some hot screwing. So once they'd come and got back aboard

116

the bed to get dressed, the mousy little gal didn't even want Longarm to escort her downstairs and out the front way.

So while he was sneaking her out a side entrance, another gal entirely was being closely watched on the far side of the tiny town.

Eva Conchita Capaz, shorter than little Cora but built far better, was coming out of the funeral parlor in the only black outfit she owned, cut frilly and trimmed with lots of Spanish lace to show the other gals in church her kin were quality folks no matter how dark their complexion or how high a lady's cheekbones might ride.

She was dabbing with a kerchief at her sloe eyes, and didn't take note of the two men observing her from the noonday shadows of a shop awning across the way. But as she sashayed past, the elder of the two rough-dressed riders whistled silently and murmured, "Moves her ass like a saloon door on payday, and Lord, I'd like to skin my dick back and shove it where the sun don't shine whilst she wags her tailbone half that fine!"

The younger one, who'd led the way to that funeral parlor across the way, muttered, "Feel free to screw anyone you want when this is over. Right now that greaser gal from Pueblo Town has been searching high and searching low for Longarm."

The older and bulkier tough went on admiring the pretty gal from the rear as he said, "Great minds run in the same channels. We've been missing him by minutes as he's been playing hopscotch all over town this morning. What makes you think she's better at tracking down nosy lawmen than us, Kid?"

The one he'd called Kid smiled wickedly and explained. "She's got a nicer ass than you, no offense, and by now she's left messages all over that she's looking for him. If we did that, we'd only make a fast draw study harder on his draw. But hearing a pretty gal is anxious to meet up with you is

117

another kettle of fish entire. The boss tells me Longarm has a rep for being as handy with the ladies as he may be with a gun, whilst that pretty little Mex gal could tempt many a preacher down the primrose path."

"I follow your drift," the older tough said. "We follow the gal till she finds Longarm. Then we give him enough rope, and as soon as he's more interested in her ass than his own back, we move in to blow his distracted head off!"

Chapter 14

By the time he'd worked his way to the last of the four books
Cora had fetched him, Longarm decided it was just as well
the mousy little thing had screwed so fine. For the privately
published books on Elbert County, while likely interesting to
members of the few proud founding families, failed to explain
what in thunder might be going on in these parts.

Longarm had already surmised, this being traditional Arapaho or South Cheyenne hunting ground, that the township of
Kiowa took its name from the creek out front, which origi-
nated as far to the south as its neighboring Box Elder Creek
from prairie springs on the higher rises called the Arkansas
Divide, closer to old-time Kiowa country.

All the Quill Indians who'd hunted buffalo this close to
Denver had been removed to reserves in the Indian Nation to
the southeast by this time, of course. The old-timers bragging about themselves in those poorly written and expensively
bound library books had come West or washed back out of the
gold country of the Front Range as both buffalo and buffalo-
hunting Indians got less common, while arable land that close
to the growing Denver market got to be more desirable. The
smaller trail town Elbert County was named for lay a good

day's cattle drive to the south. They'd decided to make the town of Kiowa the county seat because it was closer to the center of the fair-sized but thinly populated patch of rolling prairie.

One skinny book bragged on busting sod as early as '67, between the times the Third Colorado shot the liver and lights out of the South Cheyenne along Sand Creek and the Seventh Cav finished them off along the Washita. Roman Nose, the real menace this far south of Lakota country, had been turned into a "good Indian" by a rifle ball at the Beecher Island Fight about the same time. But the family journal never let on anybody from the family had missed even one of those famous battles, or massacres, depending on whether one jawed with the winners or losers.

There was nothing in any of the brags about more recent arrivals such as the Wades, Dormans, or even Sheriff Otis, although the Brandons, who'd sold out to Duke Albright and moved on, were listed as among the early pioneers of the recently incorporated county. There was no forewarning about Ed Brandon being grasshoppered out in the one book that mentioned him and his early experiment with bobwire.

Longarm got out his own notebook and listed other early homesteader names, meaning to compare them with the current county directory when and if he found the time. Old Prescott had a more complete record of improved or abandoned claims over at the land office. But it might mean something if newcomers outnumbered old-timers more than usual.

Longarm knew folks with unusually itchy feet had been the first to move West in any numbers. They said poor old Dan'l Boone had pulled stakes and moved farther west every time he spied the chimney smoke of a pesky neighbor who would likely want to borrow a cup of sugar. But it was still the general rule that a handful of folks over forty formed the core of an established township.

Meanwhile, few if any would still be out to lunch this late. So Longarm got up, had a whore-bath at the corner washstand, and got dressed again.

It was warm for April that afternoon, but not too hot to bear, and he wasn't sure when he'd get back to his baggage in the corner. So he put his denim jacket on above his gun rig, and was putting on his Stetson when there came a timid knock upon his hotel door.

It wasn't any raven bird. When the pretty little Eva Capaz asked if she'd caught up at last with El Brazo Largo, he invited her in to find out what could be making her so breathless.

Kicking the door shut—it would have been forward to shoot the bolt behind her—Longarm ushered his pretty guest in black to the window seat by the one open window on the shady side of his roomy but now half-sunbaked quarters. He wasn't surprised when she told him who she was. Somebody had to do something about that dead Diego, and there weren't that many Mexican gals with a family resemblance up this way.

But it turned out she hadn't tracked Longarm down to ask him more about her brother's drygulching. She said Jeff Wade and Skinny Pryor had both talked to her by then and each had been *muy simpatico*. So he allowed the two of them knew as much as he did about her brother's death so far, and asked if there was anything else they both had to jaw about.

Eva nodded gravely and said, "*Sí*, El Brazo Largo. My brother was not an evil person. He would not have done anything really bad. But I fear he had fallen in with *ladrones*, and that is for why somebody murdered him, I think."

Longarm, standing over her because it might have seemed forward to squeeze his butt next to her wider one on that window seat, said he'd figured Diego made more sense as the intended target than a gal nobody in Elbert County could have known that well. When he asked what else the dead vaquero's sister knew, she confided, "He wrote home just last week he might have to leave this part of the world, *poco tiempo*. He wrote he could not tell us too much on paper, but that he wanted us for to know, no matter what we might hear, he had not been *muy malo* himself. He said they had promised for to pay him *mucho dinero* for just one more job. That is what Diego called what he had been doing for someone, a job. I do not think he meant the job he had with El Señor Wade."

Longarm said he didn't think so either, and bade her go on. So she said, "Diego wrote they had not asked him to do anything *muy malo* at first. He wrote he thought they were playing jokes on some of the Anglo rancheros up this way. But then they had asked him to do more. Things that could get a *muchacho* thrown in state prison for a long time, even if he was not of our *raza*. He wrote he had told them he was only going for to help them one more time, for *mucho dinero*, and then he was coming back to Pueblo for to start his own herd over in the foothills."

She was speaking softly, despite the dramatic tale she had to tell, and Longarm was only prodding her from time to time with even softer comments. Their muffled conversation had drifted into almost pure Spanish as the two men out in the hall eased closer to the door panels to listen. The younger one, in charge, gingerly drew his six-gun as he tried the door knob with his free hand. Then he grinned up at his bulkier partner, whispering, "It's unlocked, and listen to that careless lawman talking sweet to her in there!"

The bigger tough scowled and asked, "What are they saying? Sounds like dago to me!"

The other one whispered, "Keep it down. Don't matter what you say to a greaser gal in bed if you ain't never fixing to get out of bed alive! Remember, the bed is against the wall to your left as you bust in. He's likely hung his own gun near the head of the bed, so bust in shooting and make sure you've nailed the both of 'em before you back out, lest that pesky Mex gal blabber tales about what you look like all over Creation!"

The older one frowned thoughtfully and demanded, "Ain't you busting in with me, Kid?"

The one he called Kid replied, "Boss wants me clearly visible out on the street as the famous Longarm dies in bed with a pesky greaser gal. I'm more famous here in Kiowa than you. But if it's any comfort, I stand ready to alibi you after others can alibi me. Just hit, run, and meet me in the Wagon Wheel so's I can say we was taking a piss together right about now."

The bulkier gunslick nodded grudgingly and drew his own gun. The one called Kid warned, "Give me time to get out front. Count silent to a hundred Mississippis, and remember, they'll be on the bedstead to your left as you bust in."

So the one stuck with the chore did his best to remember as he silently counted, "One Mississippi, two Mississipi, three Mississippi," at about the speed of his own heartbeats. Then he'd counted to a hundred Mississippis. He froze in buck fever for another eight or ten rapid heartbeats, and then, as he heard the man inside say something soft and comforting in Spanish, there was nothing left to do or say but fling the door open and tear in shooting as he yelled, "Powder River and let her buck!"

Then he just had time to stare in utter horror at an empty bedstead through the considerable gunsmoke of his own making before a round of .44-40 slammed into the side of his skull, spattering his brains and spreading most of him on the hall runner with his fancy Amarillo heels and silver-mounted spurs in the puddle of sunlight just inside the open doorway. He never got to hear the pretty lady scream, let alone figure out where in tarnation she and Longarm had really been all the time he was pumping lead into that unoccupied mattress.

By the time Longarm had calmed the screaming gal down, reloaded his weapon, and moved out in the hall to feel the stranger's pulse with a free hand while holding his side arm in reserve for more gunplay, the top floor was commencing to crowd up with others who seemed more astounded than out for trouble.

A kid with a tin star whom Longarm had seen with the town marshal a time or more recognized the tall federal deputy. So he lowered his own gun muzzle to ask who that might be sprawled at their feet.

Longarm holstered his own gun to open the billfold he'd found in the dead man's hip pocket. He said, "We're supposed to believe he registered to vote and took out some library books a year or so ago down San Antone way. I find it hard to buy him as the late John Bell Hood. Aside from General Hood dying about the time this jasper started to vote in his stead, the general came back from the war missing some limbs and a good ten years older than this ingenious cuss."

The young town law observed, "The death of such a Texas hero would have been in all the San Antone papers as this slicker was thinking up a new name for hisself. Them fancy Mex spurs on inlaid high-heel boots look San Antone too. As does that Texas hat against yonder baseboard all spattered with goo."

Longarm nodded down at the sprawled cadaver, and turned to call Eva Capaz out in the hall to see if she could shed light on the son of a bitch. But she just started to cry some more, and one got the impression she didn't know the dead man and didn't even want to look at him anymore. So Longarm told her to go back inside and sit until they could talk about things she did know more calmly.

A couple of townsmen in the gathering crowd had seen the dead cuss around town within the past few days. None of them

124

knew him or had any suggestions as to who might know him better.

Longarm perked up when he heard a kid dressed more cow volunteer that he'd seen the cuss, or at least a cuss wearing the same faded denim between a big Texas hat and fancy Amarillo boots, riding in from somewhere west of town aboard one of those center-fire saddles such as you saw Mexican dally-ropers favoring closer to the border.

When Longarm asked what sort of pony that saddle had been aboard, the young cowhand shrugged and said, "Nothing you'd write home about. Looked like a livery nag. Bay gelding about fifteen hands high. Eight or more years long in the tooth. He wasn't loping into town twiring a throw-rope, you understand. I'd have paid neither him or his mount that much mind if they hadn't been total strangers. All them other extra hands from other parts had been paid off for the spring roundup and had no call to hang around."

Someone else volunteered, "Oh, I dunno. We just finished the last of this year's calf-gather, and this old boy might have been looking for work when we get set for the beef-gather around August."

More than one of the locals in the crowd laughed sneeringly before the young town deputy could snort, "Oh, sure, anyone can see he was a Texican cowhand looking for honest work. That's how come he got his fool self shot in a gunfight with this federal man."

The kid who'd said he'd seen the dead man riding in on that bay gelding added, "He wasn't in these parts for the spring roundup we just had. I was. We didn't have too many outsiders for this child to remember. And who'd ever hire a dally-roping man for a Colorado calf-gather?"

Another obvious cowhand chuckled and agreed. "Damned right. The way you deal with real Colorado calves is tie-down, with a quick jerk off their feet, and they've been cut, marked, and branded before they can get their wind back. Mex dally-roping is needlessly cruel to dumb animals."

Somebody murmured something about Mexican ladies being present. The cowhand insisted, "If the truth hurts, it was never *this* child's big notion to play a calf like a fish on the line as the cutting and branding crew chases all over like they're practicing for their bullring!"

Longarm chimed in. "Never mind how this stranger to us all may or may not have roped. Can anybody tell me where his center-fire saddle and bay gelding might be right now?"

Nobody could. So Longarm asked that cowhand who'd seen the dead man riding if that bay had been branded U.S.

The kid said he couldn't say, bless his reliability. He said he'd been afoot, on the south side of the street, meaning the shoulder brand of an eastbound pony had been on its north side at the time. But he agreed the bay had looked more like an old cavalry mount than a heap of cutting ponies he'd ridden in his time.

Longarm spied the towering form of Doc Miller, the county coroner, moving his way through the confusion. It took a second longer to see Sheriff Otis was joining them as well.

He'd just finished repeating his tale to Miller and Otis when old Jeff Wade and Skinny Pryor pushed through. Longarm smiled thinly and said, "That's the trouble with small-town shootings. Everybody else in town wants to know more about them shots they just heard. Do you two know this cuss pretending to be a bear rug here?"

Jeff and his hired hand moved in for a closer look before they agreed the stranger was, by definition, a cuss they didn't know from Adam's off-ox.

Jeff asked who'd shot the ugly mutt. Longarm swore and said, "Me. Did I just ask what you're doing here in town instead of out working on that windmill, pard?"

Jeff quietly replied, "I'm here in Kiowa for conversation. Rode to the Albright spread last night to talk about my possible needs for windmills, as well as other odd notions. I told you we were aiming to, but the bully didn't seem to be home. His *segundo* and boss wrangler didn't seem to be about either. Albright's Chinee cook told us Duke was here in town."

Longarm nodded. "He was, trying to bully *me*. Before I say where I heard he'd spent the night, how serious a talk were you aiming to have with Albright, Jeff?"

The older man sounded serious enough as he quietly replied, "That's up to him. I just wanted to inform the skunk we'd cut that wire he'd strung betwixt my place and the nearest branchwater. I want to see what he says or does when I tell him we cut that fence blocking Dorman's road, along with an otherwise pointless drift fence an elderly couple has to drive clean around for no good reason at all."

Doc Miller had hunkered down to examine the dead stranger. Sheriff Otis had been paying more attention and declared, "I ain't sure I like the tone of your implied threats, Jeff Wade. I hope you know what I'll have to do to a man with a wife and family if he takes the law into his own hands."

Jeff Wade smiled innocently, but a tad wolfishly, as he told the sheriff to his face, "I ain't threatened a hair on Albright's head, Sheriff. I said it would be up to him to do whatever he means to, once I tell him what me and the few men who ain't scared of Albright did to his pesky bobwire!"

The sheriff's Oriental mustache twitched like the feelers of a spooked bumblebee as he demanded, "Is anybody here trying to say I'm scared of Duke Albright or anybody else?"

Jeff Wade shrugged and softly replied, "You've never done anything to him, or about him, no matter how we've complained to you about wide-open rawhiding!"

"I've done what you all elected me to do!" Otis protested, with a dirty look at Longarm as he continued. "You all elected me to keep the peace and uphold law and order. Unlike some I could mention, I've never been offered the chance to back anyone down in a tap room. Had I been there, nobody would have been allowed to act so childish. I'll tell Albright and his lawyer what you and your night riders have done. If they know what's good for them, they'll have it out with you all in court. I ain't about to abide with any Dodge City dramatics in a county I've been elected to ride herd on, hear?"

Skinny Pryor, standing partly behind Jeff, grumbled, "Diego Capaz was a good old boy, and they gunned that pretty Lucinda Fuller whilst you were telling us all to be so peaceable too, Sheriff."

Otis said, "I told you all then what I'm telling you all now. If anyone can show me one good reason to arrest one living soul for the killing of either one you just mentioned—"

"I thought you said you weren't scared, Mike," Jeff Wade said with a sarcastic smile.

Mike Otis snapped, "That tears it, Jeff Wade. I'm arresting you here and now for inciting to riot and sassing your own sheriff!"

Jeff Wade laughed. "You can't arrest me, Mike. I ain't *done* nothing!"

Then Otis had his Colt '74 out—he sure drew smoothly— and informed Wade more firmly he could arrest any damned body in Elbert County, and then he added Jeff could come quietly or try to fill his own fist, seeing he was feeling so ferocious of late.

Jeff stared helplessly at Longarm. "Ain't you going to tell him he can't do this, pard?"

Longarm shook his head morosely. "I can't tell him he can't do what he's obviously doing, Jeff. Take my advice and go along quiet, lest you give him more to charge you with. In the meanwhile, I'll scout up your lawyer and see if we can't get you out in time for supper, or for bed leastways."

Sheriff Otis growled, "Let's go." And so they went, even as Skinny Pryor said he'd get a lawyer called Thatcher so they could have such a fool sheriff impeached.

As half the crowd followed their sheriff and his surprise victim down the stairwell, Doc Miller rose to his own amazing height to say, "Death by gunfire. I could doubtless list it as either self-defense on your part or suicide on his. To tell the truth, I was afraid you were getting set to offer me some more business just now. Unlike that Duke Albright you backed down last night, Mike Otis means it when he puts a hand to his pistol grips!"

Longarm nodded soberly and said, "I ain't paid to beat other lawmen to the draw. Even if I was, Jeff Wade's doubtless safer under lock and key whilst I see if *I* can track down the bully of your town. For we seem to have established it that Albright doesn't want to slap leather on me. But Jeff Wade ain't me. I've seen him draw and fire at tin cans just funning after work when we rode together. He ain't bad, but he ain't good as your average gunslick, and even if he was, he ain't wearing no badge and Albright knows it."

Doc Miller nodded soberly and mused aloud, "It would be man to man, a middle-aged stockman against what I'd describe as a gunslick as well. After Jeff Wade had made public statements *he* was the one who was looking for a showdown!"

To which Longarm could only reply, "I just said that. I'd best see if I can't run Duke Albright home before old Jeff gets out of jail on a writ of habeas corpus and you wind up with another corpse to examine, Doc."

Chapter 15

First things coming first, Longarm waited until the local law had added the most recent cadaver to their collection of remains to be seen, in case anyone could identify even one of the strange gunslicks. Then he got Eva Capaz aside behind his closed door some more to tell her why she ought to head back to Pueblo pronto.

He explained, "From the way that rascal shot up yonder mattress, they were entertaining dirty thoughts about the two of us."

She blushed a becoming shade of dusky rose.

He quickly added, "I doubt they wanted to murder us over our morals. They didn't want us to share what you've already told me about your brother being in on something sneaky, doubtless with a boss sneak who just sent that poor imitation of General Hood to see the information never left this room."

The young Mexican gal protested, "I wasn't able to tell you who my brother had fallen in with or exactly what they were doing."

Longarm soberly replied, "That's what I just said. They doubtless fear your brother told you more than he did before they drygulched him. By now they figure you've surely told *me*. So I doubt you're in as much danger as me from here on, no offense."

He got out his pocket watch, saw the afternoon was half shot, and said, "They're only running that one coach both ways, so the one you came north on won't be able to take you south until tomorrow evening."

She said she'd made arrangements to have her brother's body hauled by freight wagon to the rail stop at Peyton and packed in a zinc-lined box, and meant to ride along with him.

Longarm didn't comment on the warm spell they seemed to be having. A seam of that zinc lining would give way before Pueblo or it wouldn't. He asked when she was figuring on leaving. When she said they'd told her they hoped to be ready to send Diego on his way come morning, Longarm suggested she'd be as safe and comfortable there in his hotel as anywhere else.

Her sloe eyes widened, and her face went more beet than rose before he saw he had to add, "We'll hire you another room up here on this top floor, albeit down the hall, of course."

Her features relaxed. He couldn't tell for certain whether she felt relieved or let down. He knew how he felt, knowing he'd have doubtless recovered from Cora by bedtime. But a man who really liked women as folks knew there were times when it might be best to leave a pretty little thing in mourning be.

Having settled where she'd be bedding down, Longarm had one more delicate detail to consider. When he asked her if she could use a loan to pay for expenses she and her kin might not have foreseen, Eva smiled up at him. "The things my people say about an Anglo *caballero* they call El Brazo Largo are the simple truth. *Pero* I am not from a *familia* for to be despised.

131

My brother was only playing *vaquero rustico* because he did not wish for to work in our *padre*'s machine shop with my other brothers."

So that might have ended the discussion if she hadn't finished by saying, "I am not without other friends here in Kiowa. La Señorita Redfern has been very helpful as well as *muy simpatica*."

Longarm blinked and demanded, "You turned to Lawyer Rathbone's secretary for help here in Elbert County?"

She nodded innocently. "*Sí*, my brother had mentioned her in one of his letters. He said he had asked her what he should do because he knew she was more educated about Anglo law. She told him it might be best to drop any newfound friends who asked him for to do things he thought wicked."

Longarm whistled softly. When she wanted to know what she'd said wrong, he told her, "You may have just explained more than they ever wanted anyone to spill, Miss Eva. Your brother rode for Jeff Wade. Jeff's lawyer is one William Thatcher, Esquire. Yet your brother was going to the firm of Rathbone Associates for legal advice?"

She still didn't savvy. So he explained. "Flo Redfern, pretty as she may have looked to your brother, works for Nathan Rathbone, the lawyer retained by Duke Albright, an avowed enemy of your brother's boss. Add it up."

She did. "Diego never suggested I turn to this Rathbone person, or even La Señorita Redfern. He merely wrote that he'd taken his troubles to her and that she'd told him not to do anything his own conscience told him was wrong. I do not think he told her just what those others wished for him to do. Would he have confided in even a *muy linda* one he was not related to, when he was afraid for to write all the details to us?"

Longarm said, "I fear you just answered your own question. I ain't certain how I'll ever get that snippy blonde to tell me

132

exactly what a dead cowhand confided to her in person."

Then he suggested they get cracking about hiring her another room so he could tend to some other chores.

Once they had, Longarm naturally strode over to Lawyer Rathbone's office. Flo Redfern was playing a typewriter out front, and told him right off that her boss was out of the office. "We just heard you've gunned another saddle tramp, Deputy Long. My employer is over at the courthouse trying to get a restraining order on you."

Longarm laughed incredulously and asked, "Was he really *that* upset about the way things turned out? What sort of county court order did he think might stop a federal lawman from doing what to him?"

She made a wry face and said, "Pooh, you know you've no authority to pester Nat Rathbone personally. He doesn't think you'd really be dumb enough to risk your badge by openly provoking a serious fight with Duke Albright. But our poor client seems really terrified, and so we've told him to go home and fort up, as I think you cowboys put it, until we can get your own superiors to make you behave."

Longarm snorted in disgust, and said he'd been behaving more grown-up than half the folks he'd met over this way. Then he leaned over her desk to add soberly, "I was just talking to the kin of the late Diego Capaz, another client of your firm, it would seem."

The frigidly pretty blonde shook her head and told him, "The poor boy was no such thing. Since you seem to have been fed some distorted version of our relationship, we were never lovers either. We'd met a few times, as one meets everyone in a town this size. I danced a time or two with him at the Grange Hall on chaperoned social evenings. I let him walk me home exactly once. Along the way he said he'd heard I clerked for a law firm and told me he feared he might be drifting into trouble with the law."

Longarm nodded. "Did he offer you a retainer, meaning it might be unethical for you to tell me more about the troubles of a dead client?"

She sighed and said, "Good heavens, he only walked me home from a Grange dance. He never told me exactly what he and his Anglo friends had been up to. I got the impression it involved night riding. I warned him not to make me party to a crime by confiding things I'd be duty-bound to report unless he really did retain my law firm, as you just suggested. I can assure you he never did. Based on the little he'd told me, I told him it might be a very good idea for him to finish out the month at the Wade spread and simply go home to his family in Pueblo, as he'd been thinking of doing."

It would have been rude to tell any lady he thought she was full of shit. So seeing she'd fed him a tale she doubtless didn't mean to change, Longarm gravely thanked her for clearing the matter up so simply and went back down to the street, lighting a cheroot to get the disgusted taste out of his mouth.

He strode next to the sheriff's, where he found Mike Otis and a quartet of deputies barricaded with the shotgun rack unlocked. Otis explained he'd heard talk on the street about Duke Albright making war talk about old Jeff Wade in the back.

Longarm made a wry face and dryly observed, "You'd doubtless be able to stand off Roman Nose and his whole band of Crooked Lancers. I just came from Lawyer Rathbone's office. It seems they've heard some other talk. Albright's gone home to hide under the bed. So why don't you let Jeff out now?"

Sheriff Otis shook his head stubbornly and said, "A bird in the hand is worth a gunfight Lord knows where. We heard Albright's been drinking and cussing in the Wagon Wheel, not out at his spread. So I reckon I'll just keep Jeff Wade in my fine new patent cell until some-damned-body commences to make some sense in these parts!"

Longarm didn't ask how come they hadn't locked up the bully who'd started all this bullshit. Jeff himself had allowed his own lawyer was newer at the game than the sly Nathan Rathbone, and small-town justice always seemed to favor the bigger frogs who croaked a tad more powerfully.

He shrugged, allowing at least nobody was likely to shoot his old pal, or vice versa, while he was under lock and key. Then he left to see what *he* could do about getting Jeff out.

Flo Redfern had told him her own boss lawyer was over at that nearby county courthouse pestering the court clerk, at least, for his own fool writ. So it stood to reason any lawyer worth his salt, or even young Will Thatcher, Esquire, ought to be somewhere in the same vicinity.

He spied Jeff's wife and kids in a buckboard parked out front of the dinky courthouse before he caught sight of anything that looked to be a lawyer. He naturally strode over, ticked his hat brim to her, and smiled up at the two kids as he said, "Afternoon, Miss Agatha. I take it someone's told you Jeff might not make it home in time for supper?"

The motherly Agatha Wade wearily replied, "Men! A body would think a six-shooter held the secret of eternal youth, going by the way you all seem to act as soon as you strap one on! Will Thatcher's inside with young Ekuskin as Jeff's witness, trying to make the judge see it was that silly Duke Albright, not Jeff, who started all the talk about six-shooter showdowns!"

Longarm smiled thinly and said, "I was there when the sheriff up and arrested your man, after telling him more than once to mind his manners. I suspect Mike Otis was more worried about being thought a sissy than he was about either Jeff or Duke getting hurt."

Agatha nodded. "Ekuskin told us he'd heard a lot more of our friends than just Jeff say Mike Otis was either beholden to or simply scared of Duke Albright and *his* friends."

Longarm said, "Men like Albright don't have friends. They only have enemies or boot-lickers. I suspect it's the simple fact that your Jeff is a natural leader who *has* a heap of friends that's inspired Sheriff Otis to lock him up."

Agatha asked if Longarm suspected the sheriff of being afraid of the Albright faction or in cahoots with them.

Longarm said truthfully, "I'm still working on that, ma'am. On my own time with no federal jurisdiction, unless it can be shown a local lawman is in serious violation of the federal constitution."

Then he felt obliged to add, "Before any of you ask, there ain't a thing in the Bill of Rights forbidding a sheriff up for re-election from accepting campaign contributions. How did you think the Whiskey Ring stayed out of Leavenworth during the Grant Administration? I'd only be free to step in if I caught your county or township lawmen busting a serious law for fun and profit."

She demanded, "What do you call locking up my husband, the father of these poor children, Custis?"

Little Judy sniffled and sobbed, "I want my daddy, Uncle Custis! Can't you make them give my daddy back to us?"

Before he had to tell a pretty little gal he'd never met that tooth fairy either, Skinny Pryor and a more dapperly dressed gent Longarm had never met before came out of the courthouse to join them. As Agatha did the honors and Longarm shook hands with Will Thatcher, he saw what old Jeff had meant about kid lawyers. It would have been rude to ask Agatha about it in front of Thatcher, and it was already evident that Duke Albright had hired his firm of grown-ups before Jeff had known a man just had to have a good lawyer to get by in the same county with Duke Albright.

Young Thatcher, who'd barely started shaving regular, said he knew all about Longarm and added, "First the good news.

Nat Rathbone was here earlier, trying to slap you with a restraining order. Old Judge Hollingsworth said he'd never heard a sillier suggestion for a court order than one depriving a lawman with a rep of his guns."

Skinny Pryor grumbled, "Now tell him the bad news."

Young Thatcher sighed and included Agatha Wade in his revelations as he said, "I couldn't get Jeff out on a writ of habeas corpus. As the judge seemed to be lecturing me, he's holding that I had no right to make the demand because Sheriff Otis booked Jeff properly, giving proper probable cause."

Little Judy asked if someone had made a corpse out of her daddy. Before she could bust out crying, Longarm said, "Corpus is only Latin for a body, dead or alive, honey. Lawyers talk Latin to keep the rest of us from fussing or laughing at 'em. So habeas corpus is about the same as saying Uncle Will here gets to have your daddy out of jail because Uncle Sheriff hasn't shown a good enough reason for keeping him."

Turning back to Thatcher, he asked in a more adult tone, "What's the charges, the usual suspicion based on the prisoner's own stated intent?"

Thatcher nodded. "Refusal to obey the commands of a peace officer too. Judge Hollingsworth says he thinks it might do Jeff a world of good to spend at least seventy-two hours contemplating the error of his ways."

Agatha wailed, "Oh, Lord, you mean they're fixing to hold Jeff clean through the coming weekend?"

Longarm nodded soberly and said, "Yep. That don't give me too much time to end this war before Jeff gets loose on the streets again!"

Chapter 16

Longarm didn't catch up with Duke Albright in the Wagon Wheel. So he got to hope the unreasonable bully had taken his lawyer's reasonable advice to go home and fort up, until some spoilsport had to go and say old Duke was at Riverside Saloon, down by the creek, with a skinful of redeye and songs of blood and slaughter on his lips.

Longarm knew some dumb songs too, and since half-a-dozen total assholes seemed to be tagging along to see what was going to happen next, Longarm led them all in a raucous chorus of "The Bully of the Town" as he strode down the dirt side street toward the distant tinkle of a piano playing "Lorena."

The piano left Miss Lorena waiting even longer as the boys in the Riverside heard them all coming, as he'd hoped they might, singing:

> "Oh, I am looking for the bully,
> The bully of this town,
> I am looking for the bully,
> But the bully can't be found.

So bring me out your bully,
And I'll knock your bully down.
For I am looking for the bully,
But your bully can't be found!"

A heap of Longarm's newfound admirers might have been awfully disappointed if Duke Albright hadn't been waiting in the doorway of the Riverside Saloon, asking, "You say somebody's looking for me?"

Longarm broke stride to pause at easy pistol range, his low-heeled stovepipe boots planted wide in the dusty street as he answered just as confidently, "I surely am. I ain't going into all the reasons I just don't like you, Duke. I'm a member of the human race, and we all know what you are, by your own choice. So I'm telling you to just cut it out. If you really expect to go on living here in Elbert County, or for that matter anywhere else, I want your word you'll stop pestering all your neighbors just to hear 'em holler."

Albright spat a goober into the sunbaked dust between them and sounded damned near sober, although not too bright, when he suggested a Denver queer boy try something that was as impossible as perverse, and loudly added, "I don't have to give you shit. I ain't broke one federal law. I pay a lawyer good money to make sure I never do. So what are you going to do if I just tell you to go soak your head in a bucket of warm spit, Longarm?"

It was a good question, and a fair one, to hear the murmur all around as Albright sneered, with growing confidence, "You're not man enough to run this child out of his own town! Nat Rathbone explained to me what you pulled on me in that hotel tap room. You were bluffing, plain and simple. You knew I'd have had to be clean out of my head to draw on a federal lawman in front of witnesses. So you just tried to make me look bad by daring me to draw."

Longarm mildly suggested, "Why don't you go for your gun now if you think I'm bluffing?"

Albright grinned as only a drunk who thinks he has the secret of the universe at last can grin. "It ain't going to work this time. I am stating here and now in front of God and Kiowa Township that I ain't afraid of the high and mighty Longarm. I just know better than to let him push me up a tree I can't climb down from."

Turning slightly to address the gathering crowd, as if he thought he was Mark Antony or someone as slick, Albright loudly declaimed, "He knows he'd have the right to put me in jail or even murder me if I was dumb enough to slap leather on a lawman in front of witnesses. Knowing I'm too smart and pretty, with too much to lose, he's here today playing hero. But anyone with a lick of sense can see this is only a Mexican standoff, with neither side fixing to make the first unlawful move!"

Longarm stepped closer, declaring more politely, "Whether you call my bluff or not, Duke, Jeff Wade's getting out again sooner or later, and I doubt like hell he'll come bluffing. You really made him mad when you set his friends, the Dormans, on fire."

Duke Albright sneered, "Let anyone who says that *prove* it! I don't care what Jeff Wade thinks. I ain't afraid of him neither. This child ain't afraid of any man in Elbert County!"

As if to prove this he threw back his head, crowed a wild border rooster laugh, and announced, "Cockeedoodledoo and I'll shove my cock in you! I'm tough and gruff and up to snuff and all my women like it rough. So I'll take on your mama if you ain't enough!"

Longarm said quietly, "We'd best leave our kinfolk out of this."

But then Albright was dancing back and forth on the saloon's plank walk, chanting, "You daddy's a pimp and your mother's a whore. What will you do if I tell you some more? You're nothing but a bushel of talk, so fill your fist or take a walk!"

Everyone but Longarm seemed to find this mighty amusing. The tall deputy considered just stepping up on those planks with the annoying asshole to pistol-whip some manners into him. But he suspected that was just what Albright wanted him to do. It was becoming ever clearer why Jeff and his more rational friends just didn't *like* this crazy-mean son of a bitch. But it could be dumb to just act natural around such a dedicated candidate for martyrdom. Longarm knew all too well how much trouble a lawman could get into for abusing his powers under the current reforms of President Hayes. He had reason to suspect Albright knew that too. He'd just bragged on being coached by a slick lawyer on such points of the law.

So it hurt like fire, but there was nothing half as smart a lawman could do but turn and walk away as all those men and boys gasped in astonishment, before they started laughing like hell.

He let them have their laugh at his expense, hoping to have the last one if ever he fathomed what in thunder was going on. Back in the tap room at his hotel he found the crowd less uncouth, although those few who'd already heard seemed to have a time meeting Longarm's eyes, as if they felt embarrassed for him.

Seth Mathis was there with his grown son, Shem. They were worried about Albright and his riders really acting up with Jeff Wade locked up for whole weekend.

As Longarm sipped beer at the bar with them, he mildly observed they had a paid-up sheriff of their own choosing.

Young Shem Mathis snorted, "Until next November, you mean. Mike Otis might as well go to work direct for Duke Albright, seeing he seems to be on the range hog's payroll in any case."

Longarm didn't ask if anyone could prove Sheriff Otis corrupt. An elected official perceived by the voters as such was likely to lose whether he really was or not. So Longarm suggested, "Let's talk about range-hogging. Your county agent and me were trying to figure a method to Albright's crazy-mean ways over to the land office. It's a fact he's managed to gain title to many a quarter section out yonder. But there's a hell of a lot of yonder out yonder. It's one thing to cut a particular neighbor off from water or an established right-of-way. It's another kettle of fish to become more than a petty pain in the ass to a limited number."

Seth Mathis grumbled, "Tell that to Silas Dorman, tied up in court for a coon's age over that pointless fence and empty ditch betwixt his claim and the post road!"

Longarm said, "I just now tried to make that point. Sooner or later the case has to come to trial, and once it does, Dorman is sure to win. Albright doesn't own that strip of public land he's taken it into his fool head to abuse that way, and even if he did, Dorman would doubtless be granted an easement by the court. That's what you call it when you've been using a passageway across public or private land for more than an undisputed year, an easement. As a matter of common law you don't have the right to stop folks from using an established right-of-way, even if you own the land it cuts across."

Young Shem demanded, "So how come we had to cut that fool fence and fill in that fool ditch for the Dormans our ownselves?"

"You boys seem to have been less patient than the wheels of county justice. Jeff would have likely won the right to water his stock in that nearby branchwater in court, if he hadn't cut corners and just given Lawyer Rathbone an opening by taking the law into his own hands with wire cutters. Riparian or water rights are a lot like rights-of-passage under common law. As far back as Roman times it was easy to see you'd only have heaps of trouble if you let some total-ass stranger cut off someone's babbling brook just by gaining title to its banks upstream. There's a whole shit-house of riparian laws designed to prevent just the sort of fussing Duke Albright seems to enjoy so much."

Seth Mathis nodded soberly. "Now that you mention it, Jeff and some of the others have allowed Mike Otis could just tell the ornery cuss to cut it out, if he really wanted to."

Fair was fair, so Longarm said, "I just came from asking Duke Albright to act more neighborly. I'll be switched with snakes if I can see how anyone so loco could wind up so rich. Sheriff Otis may be puzzled as me as to what the real game might be. Prescott, over at the land office, suggested some half-ass plan to gain control of a sort of bar sinister of prairie, followed by some demands for passage tolls. I suspect Albright hails from Texas if you track him backwards, and he may have heard how Chief Quanah Parker demands and collects a toll on cattle crossing his Comanche Reserve."

Young Shem Mathis asked, "Wouldn't that wild notion come under them rights-of-passage easements you just mentioned?"

Longarm nodded, told Seth Mathis he'd raised a bright kid, and said, "I said it was a half-ass plan, if that's the plan. Prescott and me agreed nobody who really savvied country matters would try to gobble up such wide-open country a quarter section at a time. It would be like a mouse trying to eat out a grain elevator grain by grain by grain."

Young Shem opined, "Never thought Duke Albright was much of a cattleman, for all his swagger and silver-mounted saddle. He barely grazes enough stock on all that range he's messed up with fencing to keep the weeds down. Anybody who knows cows knows you want your herd grazing widespread enough to let the short-grass recover, but tight enough to discourage anything else from sprouting."

His father nodded and said, "Seen some cottonwood shoots on high ground along one of them new fence lines of Albright's just about a week ago. Stock has to be grazing fat and lazy to pass up any juicy cottonwood shoots in greenup time!"

Skinny Pryor came in through the swinging doors to tell Longarm that Miss Agatha and the Wade kids were fixing to drive home for now, and that Miss Agatha still had that guest room and a place at their supper table waiting for him.

Longarm knew it would be impolite to turn down such an invitation by way of hired help. So he allowed he'd tell Miss Agatha personally, and explained to Skinny along the way how he had to ride down to Peyton with Eva Capaz and her brother's body come morning.

Skinny grinned and said, "Some old boys have all the luck. I got to help Miss Agatha around the spread, as short-handed as all their troubles have left them. I talked to Diego's pretty sister over to the funeral parlor this very morn. She sure looked as if she could use a little cheering up."

Longarm didn't answer. He wasn't sure who he wanted to know his real reasons for availing himself of the Western Union facilities at the larger railroad stop. He didn't know for a fact that anyone working for Western Union here in Kiowa made a habit of gossiping with the courthouse gang. He only knew he meant to play his cards a tad close to his vest until such time as he figured out who might be up to what in these parts.

As they stepped out on the walk, Skinny was asking which of the Wade ponies Longarm wanted him to leave at the nearby livery. When he explained his boss had told him to run most of the stock on home to cut down on their livery bill, Longarm said to take them all. He had his saddle and such upstairs in the hotel, and could hire all the riding stock he might need once he saw he needed it.

Skinny started to say something about that long ride down to the rail line with Eva Capaz. But by then they'd rejoined Agatha and her kids out front and Longarm was graciously declining her kind offer of free room and board, saying he wanted to stay closer to the action.

Agatha sighed down at him, pleading, "See if you can talk my man into leaving law and order to you lawmen, Custis. I just told him it's not lawful or even sensible to take the law into your own hands. But you know how upset that silly Duke Albright has made so many of our menfolk."

Longarm said he'd try and have a word with Jeff and maybe get some tobacco to him later that evening. Agatha said she'd already fetched him tobacco and a mess of magazines, along with a pound of rock candy. But then she added, "You might be the one person my Jeff would listen to, Custis. We've followed your career in both the *Denver Post* and *Rocky Mountain News* over the years, and your ears would have been burning if you'd heard my man brag on knowing you."

Little Judy volunteered, "My daddy says you roped good and faced down the Thompson brothers in some place called a Long Branch, Uncle Custis. What's a Long Branch and how do you face a brother down?"

Her mother nudged her to make her hush. But Longarm told the child her daddy had just been funning about a kid cowhand he'd taken under his wing one time.

Agatha said quietly, "That showdown in Dodge was more recent, and Jeff told us how handy it was to be able to call on an experienced lawman who knew more than most about the cattle industry. He's often said he'd have likely gone along with you to ride for Billy Vail and the law if I hadn't roped and hog-tied him so young."

Longarm laughed lightly and allowed her Jeff had always been a joshing man. Women hated to think they'd held a man back from running off to sea or growing up to be a railroad engineer, even when it was true.

Young Shem Mather had drifted out of the tap room to take in the last half of the conversation. So as Agatha drove off, with Skinny headed over to the livery to catch up with her later, Shem stated flatly, with the sureness of a youth who still had a heap of dumb mistakes to make, "I don't aim to marry up before I'm dead certain what I mean to be by the time I'm thirty or so. Do you reckon Jeff really means to go down in history as the man who shot Duke Albright, leaving a wife and two kids as he mounts them thirteen steps to the gallows?"

Longarm stared soberly after the receding buckboard as he softly replied, "I don't know. I thought I knew more than I did until a few minutes ago. But Duke Albright's too smart to be suckered into making the first move. So it would be tough enough for a paid-up lawman to gun him halfway legal."

Shem suggested, "I follow your drift. But even packing his six-gun low and tie-down, he'd have to feel awfully brave to give Jeff the first move, wouldn't he?"

Longarm shrugged and said, "You may have just answered your own question, Shem. I've seen old Jeff draw and fire. He's about average. If he went up against a real gunslick packing a side arm any old way, I'd hate to have my money riding on Jeff!"

Chapter 17

The drive south with Eva Capaz was twenty-odd miles shorter than Longarm's snowy trip from Denver with poor Lucinda Fuller. It was a mite different in other ways as well.

The moody April climate of the High Plains remained in a bright and sunny mood, with the grass green as clover and the first pasqueflowers opening their big blue eyes hither and yonder. Longarm and his old McClellan saddle were aboard a paint mare that old Arapaho at the livery swore he'd almost married up with before her family objected to his complexion. Eva rode on the freight wagon with the two-man crew and her dead brother. His zinc-lined coffin had to share the wagon bed with some green hides and spring radishes bound for the railroad stop at Peyton. The freight wagon, like the local stage and that hotel back in Kiowa, was part of the shrinking but still fairly spread-out Overland empire of Mister Ben Holladay. He called you a sissy if you called him Benjamin.

His rivals running Wells Fargo described the tall and husky Ben Holladay as "energetic, untiring, unscrupulous, and wholly destitute of honesty, morality, or common decency." But his freight crew treated the pretty Mexican gal and her dead brother politely enough. So the day's drive went smoothly, although it was tedious as hell.

Despite the winks and suggestions of others, and his own masculine desires, Longarm knew Mexican gals felt just as morose about dead brothers as anyone else. So when they got to Peyton, they just shook hands and parted like quality folks once he and the Overland crew made sure she and old Diego were on their way by rail to Pueblo.

After a couple of beers with the old boys he'd ridden with all day, Longarm was free to find another livery for the paint and a hired room for the night in what they laughingly described as a hotel. The freight platform and loading chutes, over by the railroad siding, were about the most impressive structures in the town of maybe a hundred souls. But nobody at the Peyton Western Union was likely to be having a beer with anyone from Kiowa in the near future. So Longarm felt far more carefree as he sent wires of inquiry all over Creation.

One he sent to a certain cattle queen down Texas way left a man who'd slept alone the night before feeling sort of wistful. But he figured a horny beauty who dealt in every Texican commodity from beef to cotton and slash-pine turps would surely know if anyone had ever made an honest dollar down yonder under the name of Albright. He described all those dead men dressed sort of border *buscadero* to a Ranger captain he was on somewhat less intimate terms with. Then he wired old Henry, the clerk who played the typewriter and kept up the files in their Denver office, to see if they had any new flyers that a single one of the bastards might fit.

Having done that much, and having even found a sit-down place near the tracks to eat supper, Longarm was stuck with the simple fact that a Saturday night in a town like Peyton could turn out mighty tedious.

But fortunately the one waitress, who'd been stuck there a good spell longer, had already noticed that. Her name was Rose, she got off at nine, and while she was only pretty when she smiled, she smiled a lot at Longarm as they got to know one another better, in her beanery for quite a few extra cups of coffee, and later up in his hotel room once she felt free to drag him outside and confess she'd been waiting for him forever in that dusty railroad stop in the middle of the Great American Desert.

He found this easier to believe once they were undressed in bed together, with her on top and begging him not to stop as she did all the work.

It felt so good he spent the next thirty-odd hours in her mighty pleasant company. She didn't have to work on the Sabbath, he had to give others the time to reply to his wires, and what the hell, they had Jeff Wade safely locked away until Monday afternoon at least.

A Rose by any other name might have had more to say when the two of them weren't eating, sleeping, or fornicating. But there was something to be said for fornicating with amiable half-wits once the time came to move on. He was braced for at least the plea that he write her a letter now and again. But when he told her he just hated to tear himself away, but had to heed the call of duty, Rose just asked if they had time for a quick one, and seeing they sure did, suggested he look her up again if ever he came back this way.

It was funny how odd it made a man feel, being dropped like some old used-up cigar butt after putting all that effort into an easy gal.

He made better time riding back to Kiowa, starting well before dawn Monday morning. Livery nags were always more willing to lope on home than they were to lope on out. And he wanted to be sure he was there when they let Jeff Wade out that afternoon.

He rode in before the county courts would be open for business, having spent better than three hours in the saddle with the courthouse gang keeping banker's hours. But even showing up on the same day could be slicing things thin, so he rode direct to the jail, tethered the jaded paint out front, and strode in to see if old Jeff had calmed down some after three nights away from good old Agatha's cooking and other talents.

Sheriff Otis wasn't in yet. The deputy at his desk told Longarm he'd arrived too late to visit that particular prisoner. He reached for a ledger, but said, "We let 'em out late Saturday afternoon as I recall."

Longarm gasped. "Jesus H. Christ! How come?"

The county lawman turned to the recent entry and calmly replied, "Had to. Big Denver lawyer called Heinz got a state superior court to wire Will Thatcher a writ. Sheriff Otis was a tad startled by it as well, come to study on it."

Longarm said, "I should think we'd all be! Lawyer Heinz in Denver is a known associate of Nathan Rathbone, Esquire, Duke Albright's lawyer here in Kiowa!"

The deputy didn't seem to follow Longarm's drift. Longarm said he'd ask Will Thatcher, and demanded, "Have they had it out yet, or has Otis been able to somehow keep the peace?"

The deputy frowned thoughtfully, nodded, and declared, "There was some talk of a Saturday night shootout, now that you call it to mind. But we never had one. Only trouble we had all night was Luke Cheeseman, in the back, sleeping off a drunk and disorderly after a fall that should have busted his fool neck."

Longarm was already halfway out the door, his mind in a whirl as he thought about what *could* have happened as he lay slugabed, or at least in bed, with old Rose a good twenty miles away!

He untethered and remounted to lope the slow but steady paint over to Will Thatcher's, asking directions along the way.

He found the kid lawyer and his pretty young wife having breakfast in the kitchen, served by the colored gal their social stature called for. Felicia Thatcher didn't seem embarrassed to be seen eating eggs in a quilted kimono, and invited Longarm to join them for breakfast as soon as her husband introduced them. So Longarm figured she'd been raised by honest country folk, and hadn't gotten snooty just because she'd married up with a gent who put on a fresh white shirt every day.

The scrambled eggs and Canadian bacon hit the spot after a long lope through the morning chill, and he said so. Then he just had to ask Lawyer Thatcher how in thunder he'd ever gotten one of Albright's powerful lawyers to pull such serious strings for an avowed enemy of his own client.

Thatcher looked sheepish and confessed, "I didn't do a thing. I don't know Abe Heinz from the Tsar of All the Russians, and I hear Heinz feels he's at least that important. But when a state superior court grants a client of mine a writ of habeas corpus, I take it!"

Longarm demanded, "Knowing said client has sworn he means to have it out with a born bully who's even wilder?"

Thatcher's face flushed, but he managed to keep his voice as calm when he replied in a tone of sweet reason, "Ours not to reason why. Your lawyer's supposed to get you *out* of trouble after you get *into* it. The only way to prevent clients from ever getting into trouble would be to lock them up at birth and never let them out."

Felicia dimpled and demanded, "What are the two of you arguing about, for heaven's sake? There wasn't any gunfight. I don't see how there's supposed to *be* a gunfight now that Jeff Wade's run Duke Albright out of Elbert County!"

Longarm shot a puzzled frown at her husband, who nodded and told him, "Looks like it. I warned Jeff he ought to go right home and let the law take its course with an obvious lunatic. But have you ever argued with the north wind in January?"

Longarm said, "I know Jeff can be set in his ways. What happened?"

Thatcher shrugged and said, "Nothing, just as Lisha says. Jeff got out before sundown, strapped on his gun, and headed over to that Riverside Saloon to see if Albright was still there. When he discovered Albright wasn't at the Wagon Wheel or that tap room Nat Rathbone prefers to drink at, Jeff and some of his pals saddled up to ride out to Albright's home spread."

"Nobody was home!" Felicia chimed in brightly, waving their hired gal over to pour more coffee as her husband nodded. "Not even the boss wrangler. As far as anyone can tell, Albright and his boys pulled up stakes and lit out, like thieves in the night, as soon as they heard someone with no political strings holding him back was ready to just have it out man to man!"

Longarm whistled softly and declared, "I'm sure glad I ain't Mike Otis, having to run for office again come November. I don't see how I'd explain anything that simple-sounding to the voters. For to tell the truth, I thought Duke Albright had more sand in his craw than *that*."

He'd left the wires he'd gotten so far in his saddlebag out back.

He said so, but added, "I've wired high and I've wired low without being able to get a solid line on Duke Albright, albeit more than one Texas pal suggests he must have made his money some other place or under some other name. The Texas Rangers were not amused to hear a sinister stranger had lost a fight under the name of their own General Hood. They think he could have been a jasper they knew better as one Leroy Longstreet, not related to *that* Confederate hero either but really a Longstreet on his certificate of baptism. So what we have, on the face of it, is a fair-sized bunch of big bad Texicans who horn into a Colorado county, pester folks, scare

152

'em all skinny, and then run away like a bunch of sissies as soon as a real man stands up to them?"

Felicia Thatcher smiled uncertainly at Longarm, saying, "I'm sure you're a real man, Deputy Long. Yet didn't at least some of them have the nerve to fight *you*?"

To which Longarm could only modestly reply, "That's about the size of it, ma'am. I find it sort of confusing too."

Thatcher asked when Longarm would be heading back to Denver, seeing the emergency seemed about over.

Longarm didn't want to swear in front of a woman, so he only stated firmly, "It ain't over. Somebody has to answer for a lady called Cindy and a cowhand called Diego. I may not have the jurisdiction over such local matters as hayloft burning, but Lucinda Fuller and Diego Capaz were murdered in the first degree on a federal post road across federal open range."

The young lawyer and his wife exchanged glances. As she buttered Longarm more toast her husband said, "Nobody's ever suggested your badge doesn't cover a lot of ground, Deputy Long. But try it this way. Say Duke Albright was the mean rich kid Jeff Wade kept saying he was. Say he hired others to do his real fighting for him. Then, thanks to you and Jeff, say all the real fighting men got themselves shot up, leaving one boss bully with only his brag and a handful of help no tougher than he was."

Longarm nodded soberly and replied, "I've already considered all you just said. Some of it works. After that I'm stuck with a rascal rich and mean enough to hire at least three gunslicks and send 'em out to murder folks. If they were the ones who killed Cindy and Diego, so be it. But a man mean and rich enough to hire three gunslicks hither could likely find as many more yonder. Which has to make more financial sense than simply abandoning all that land and livestock without any struggle at all!"

Lawyer Thatcher suggested, "Unless one was afraid a smart lawman was about to uncover something that made running sound way smarter!"

Longarm sighed and said, "Oh, Lord, I wish I was half as smart as everyone keeps saying I am!"

Chapter 18

A man needed neither a mount nor all that much boot leather to get around Kiowa. So Longarm took the hired paint back to the town livery, and toted his saddle and such back to the only hotel in the tiny town. They hired him the same room, although with a much fresher mattress on the bedstead and a brand-new runner down the hall outside his door.

The Western Union office he'd gone to all that trouble to avoid was a one-room shack just down the way. He didn't get the argument he expected from the ginger-haired one-man crew. The clerk had no trouble with a federal lawman's request for private information because nobody of any description had wired any lawyer at all over Denver way for the past ten days. The clerk said they discarded all but a few mighty important-looking telegram blanks within that many days. He naturally had a copy of the wire *from* Denver, telling Otis he had no just cause to hold Jeff Wade. But when Longarm got to read it, he saw nothing he hadn't already been told. The superior court clerk in Denver who'd sent the wire stated the motion for the plaintiff, Wade, had been brought by the Denver law firm of Heinz & Heinz on Larimer Street.

Figuring Lawyer Rathbone had sent his own message from another telegraph office within a day's ride in most any direction, Longarm strode over to the slippery rascal's law office to tell him so.

Rathbone hadn't come in yet, or so said his ash-blond *segunda*, Flo Redfern. She sounded sincere and almost worried as she assured Longarm she hadn't seen her boss since Friday noon, and added with a sigh she hadn't been paid that evening as expected.

Longarm frowned thoughtfully and decided, "Not having your lawyer around to bail you out could inspire even a dim-witted bully to avoid a showdown. After that it starts to sound more complicated."

He paused to choose his words with care before he smiled thinly down across her desk at her. "I know all about that privileged-information principle of common and constitutional law. Lawyers keep pulling it on me all the time, and there's things you can't even get out of a lawyer at the point of a court order, lest you blow your own side out of the water by offering grounds for an appeal to a higher court. So I ain't asking you anything about anybody as their attorney of record. I'm a federal lawman questioning a witness who just don't *have* no standing with the Colorado Bar Association to back her play if she gets arrested for withholding information about a felony."

The cool blonde met his gaze with a pretty poker face and blandly asked what felony they could be talking about.

He chuckled sheepishly and said, "You ought to have your own law degree. You're good. I'll allow I just don't know what in thunder a mysterious cattle baron and even his lawyer expect to get caught at. But it's got to be mighty serious. Would you abandon land, cows, or even this here building Albright owns unless you were dead certain it could cost you more to sit tight?"

She objected that she'd heard nothing about anybody abandoning a single thing. She let a little steel creep into her dulcet tones as she demanded he quit pussyfooting and either make some charges or forever hold his peace.

Longarm nodded down at her and stated, "If you'd been in on it they'd have taken you with them, or at least paid you off before they asked you to hold the fort and fend off questions like mine as long as possible. You're still no more than an office worker, without a real lawyer's immunity. So I'll ask you one more time what you know about your boss pulling strings to get the sworn enemy of his richer main client out of jail!"

She shook her pinned-up head and insisted, "I'm not refusing to tell anybody. I simply don't *know*. Nat Rathbone didn't say a word to me about Jeff Wade or strings. I haven't seen him since before the sheriff arrested Mister Wade Friday afternoon! Why don't you ask Abe Heinz or that Denver judge who issued the writ? They'd surely know more than me!"

Longarm grimaced and said, "Aw, come on. You just heard me say you were good. Does that make me a greenhorn who just got off a boat in New York Harbor? We both know how judges and lawyers laugh when a poor working badge-toter asks them questions they don't have any call to answer."

He looked past her at the closed door of Rathbone's inner office as he grumbled, "I respect motherhood and the Bill of Rights as much as the next lawman. But there are times I wonder how many of those lawyers who whipped up our constitution had heaps of clients who had heaps of mighty dirty laundry!"

She started to give him a prim-lipped lecture on the need for client-attorney confidences. He said he'd heard it, added he'd be over to the hotel if she really wanted to see some justice in these parts, and left.

Feeling sort of like one of those wooden chargers on some fool merry-go-round, Longarm strode back the way he'd started to see if Sheriff Otis was in yet.

Mike Otis was, twirling one end of his mandarin mustache in his own puzzled way as he allowed it surely seemed as if Duke Albright and all but a few bewildered house and stable hands had lit out in a hell of a hurry for parts unknown.

Longarm said he suspected Lawyer Rathbone was missing as well, and added, "This is your county, and I'm only here on my own vacation time. So it would be best if you were to put out an all-points by wire."

Otis scowled. "An all-points saying what? Am I supposed to charge Albright with avoiding a fight, or his lawyer with riding off to gather pasqueflowers on the prairie?"

Longarm said, "They never headed en masse for the rail stop to the south. They could have made Denver on horseback easy over the weekend, and Rathbone's in thick with some Denver lawyers who seem to have pals around the state court on Capitol Hill."

Otis shrugged. "*You* wire Denver then. I say good riddance to the both of 'em, and I ain't about to make a sap out of myself by wiring all over as if I was playing Little Bo Peep with black sheep!"

So Longarm went back to the damned Western Union and sent the damned wires himself. He knew better than to charge anyone with anything before he knew what they were running from. But old Henry at the home office and his pal Sergeant Nolan of the Denver P.D. were in better position than he was to say whether all those jaspers had even passed through Denver on their way to other parts.

After a well-deserved noon dinner, Longarm took those four books back to the library. He'd promised to return them, and you just never knew whether a modest maiden might have changed her mind. But when he got there he found the older one, Miss Hamilton, in charge. She took back the fool books with a smile. But she looked a lot like an army mule in a gingham dress, and while an ugly old gal might be able to give a man half as much pleasure in bed, she cost him twice as much pain if she turned him down. So he took the advice of the younger of the two library gals and quit while he was ahead.

The afternoon was even more tedious, and the night that followed was a bitch. But a manhunter didn't quit just because he had no idea what in thunder he thought he was doing.

Chapter 19

Longarm spent the next morning asking hundreds of questions without getting one damned answer that shed any light on the puzzle.

Longarm couldn't buy the simple solution everyone seemed out to sell him. The notion that his old pal Jeff Wade had simply said, "Boo!" to send a big bully and his slick lawyer packing made little or no sense as soon as anyone thought back to all the earlier threats, lawsuits, and such that Duke Albright and his pals had just laughed off.

Longarm wasn't low-rating a friend when he reminded folks how Duke hadn't been afraid to stand up to a lawman with a modest rep and his own six-gun. But more than one old-timer dismissed that notion by pointing out that nobody expected any peace officer to draw on a man who refused to fight, while a thoroughly pissed Jeff Wade made for a far less certain proposition!

Getting nowhere with folks who knew even less than he did, Longarm struck color, if not pay dirt, rummaging through dusty files in desperation at the county clerk's.

Storming back up to Rathbone's office, he found Flo Redfern still holding the fort and demanded, "How come you never told me old Duke Albright was incorporated? Were you figuring to spring that on poor Silas Dorman after he won that easement case against a client the other side had down as an individual property owner?"

The cool blonde smiled smugly and demurely replied, "We're not required to volunteer information like that. Had we been seriously trying to hide it, how come you found it so easily just now?"

Longarm snapped, "I never found it easy. It was buried in the files, under a heap of other papers you all filed along with it to confuse the issue. You had to file *some* incorporation papers because that's the way you incorporate a slippery dealer so no matter what he pulls, you can only sue and collect from his corporation."

She repressed a polite yawn and asked why he was lecturing her on basic business law.

He said, "Mayhaps I'm lecturing me, to get it straight in my own less crooked head. It still adds up to Kansas Ferguson and some other pals being listed as junior partners in Albright Land and Cattle Associates, Incorporated."

She shrugged and said, "I know. I typed up the application forms."

He nodded soberly. "In that case you likely noticed your *own* name, along with that of Lawyer Rathbone, on the list of incorporated shareholders. I was adding in my head, but unless I was way off, no one individual owns the better than fifty percent of the shares it would take to steer the ship without asking anyone else. So how do you like a heap of shareholders suddenly up in a magical puff of fairy dust, leaving all that land and beef on the hoof to . . . Who's left, aside from you your ownself, Miss Flo?"

The ash-blonde went even paler as she protested, "Surely you're not serious, Deputy Long! I only work here. They only asked me to be a small cog in the corporate wheels because, to be frank, the more the merrier when you're setting up a dummy corporation."

When he just went on staring down at her, she licked her lips and tried, "You surely saw I hold a less than ten-percent interest in Albright Incorporated!"

Longarm shrugged. "That's more than *I* own. I'd say *any* percent gives you more control over the considerable property than anyone else I can find right now in these parts!"

She rose from her desk, almost wailing, "You're not going to frame me on some trumped-up charge, damn your smug smile! I just told you my boss hasn't even paid me for two weeks, and this will make it the third if he doesn't get back before Friday!"

Longarm went on smiling as he answered simply, "Wasn't talking about wages in arrears, ma'am. Talking about everyone but one minor shareholder of a going concern having vanished into thin air. How would you read that if *you* were sitting on a grand jury?"

She looked as if she was fixing to cry. Longarm told her to think about it and get word to him later if she had anything else to tell.

He left her to stew alone, and enjoyed a *Police Gazette* and a haircut while he waited for his pals in Denver to wire back. He resisted going back to the Western Union before it was going on supper time. When he did, Sergeant Nolan had wired that a dozen-and-a-half horses had been left, saddles and all, tethered out front of Union Station much too long with neither fodder nor water. They'd been taken to the municipal pound until somebody claimed them or figured what to do with them, and yes, more than one of them had been branded Lazy A. Longarm had asked Nolan to watch for that, seeing that was Duke Albright's registered brand.

Henry had wired he'd been jawing to no avail with his opposite number at the state superior court. The priss didn't know or just couldn't say what Lawyer Heinz had on the judge who'd issued that writ. Longarm found it tough to buy that whole bunch stampeding off like that because one reasonably firm stockman might come looking for them. It was even tougher to figure how a cruel-hearted woman had done away with all her business partners at once, leaving their riding stock tethered miles away by a railroad depot!

Knowing he'd done all the easy legwork in town, Longarm turned in early with plenty of smokes and some reading material, hoping to dream up some sensible destination for the early start he meant to get in the morning. So he was stretched out on the bedstead in just his shirt, jeans, and socks, when he heard gentle rapping and got up to discover Flo Redfern standing there. A strand of blond hair had come unpinned, and she looked as if she'd cried a lot since last they'd spoken. Her worried eyes were all red-rimmed, and as he ushered her to that window seat she told him, "I've just come from Nat Rathbone's quarters. His housekeeper says she hasn't seen him since Friday morning either!"

Longarm shut the door and trimmed the lamp by the bedstead to almost plunge them into total darkness. As she gave a startled gasp he assured her, "Don't want to shutter that window on such a balmy evening. Don't want anyone shooting either of us from outside either. Your eyes will adjust in a minute, and I have some good news for you."

He moved closer, but didn't sit beside her in the narrow space as he continued. "It wasn't bad news leastways. A whole mess of your corporate shareholders seem to have hopped a train out of Denver over the weekend. Denver P.D. recovered many a head of Lazy A riding stock by the Union Depot. After that it gets mysterious as ever. I used to ride with Jeff Wade. I've seen him handle his end of a saloon fight when our world was a tad younger and sillier. Jeff's all right. But I can't see a dozen grown men acting *that* scared of him. So whether it sounds like bragging or not, they lit out right after I dropped out of sight over the same weekend. How do you like the notion somebody added two and two to get seven or eight?"

She suddenly reached out to grab one of his hands and cling to it as if she thought it a straw as she almost sobbed, "I'm scared! I don't want to be blamed for things I've never done! I'm even less anxious to have them done to me! I think somebody has done something just awful to Nat Rathbone. He'd never just run off and leave like that. I've been thinking of what you said, about it being smarter to pay me my wages as usual before announcing an innocent business trip. He's gone into Denver on many such trips since I've been working for him here in Kiowa. That would have been the smart way to get far and wide before anyone knew he was missing, and Deputy Long, he has never struck me as a stupid man!"

Longarm quietly suggested, "My friends call me Custis," even as he idly wondered why she was rubbing her cheek against the back of that hand, like a kitten trying to make friends in a hurry.

He said, "A client who'd done something mighty mean to his lawyer on a Friday would doubtless want to be some-wheres else come Monday. But they were supposed to be pals and business partners and . . . Why are you feeling yourself up with my hand, Miss Flo?"

She went on rubbing his hand against the front of her thin lemon and lime bodice as she replied in a husky tone, "I'm just feeling all alone and afraid, I guess. Don't you like it? Do you want me to stop?"

He hauled her to her feet and got an even nicer grip on her shapely body, noting she didn't have anything on under that summer-weight dress, as he replied, "You ain't alone. You're with me. I know they told you it would compromise any lawman who arrested you in court if you let him have some slap and tickle before or after he arrested you. But I don't care if you compromise me or not, you pretty little slicker."

So she kissed him eagerly, and moaned, "Oh, Custis, what are you *doing* down there?" as he compromised himself good with two fingers between her firm young buttocks while he picked her up to carry her the few steps to the bedstead.

Thanks to neither of them having all that much to shuck, they got to enjoy their first shared climax naked, atop the bedding, as the evening breeze through the open window inspired his bare rump to gallantry she found inspiring. He said she moved her willowy torso awfully nice as well. He didn't ask any more questions, or even talk to her all that much before he'd made her come more than once and lit up a cheroot for them to share, propped up so bare and friendly against the headboard. And so, just as he'd hoped, she got around to telling him all she knew, stroking his limp organ-grinder as she did so, even though he kept telling her she sounded innocent enough so far.

He'd have never made love to her to begin with if he'd really been expecting to arrest her. As she relaxed in his arms and opened up to him in more ways than one, he saw how some, if not all, of the tangled foolishness had been supposed to work. He assured her nobody but a sort of Eastern dude lawyer could have ever come up with such a harebrained plot, and muttered, "They all want to *play* Machiavelli without *reading* Machiavelli! The first thing old Nick warns you to do is make certain you know what you're doing!"

She seemed to know just what to do to a lover's semierection as she calmly replied the master plan had made perfect sense to *her*.

He gripped their cheroot between his bared teeth and reached down to return the favor with his own skilled fingers as he gently allowed he'd never figured her for a cowgirl. He said, "As I see what your missing boss thought he was doing, he'd set up this dummy land and cattle corporation, with his real controlling majority lost in them other papers I should have looked at closer, right?"

She purred, "Yes. Faster. You do that so fine, Custis!"

He went on strumming her bitty pink banjo as requested, but told her, "It would have never worked the way he planned. Getting a born bully he'd domesticated with flattery and pocket jingle to front for him got a heap of real stockmen upset, even made some few sell out to Rathbone, thinking it was Albright, but they never in this world could have gotten that stranglehold on this range your boss bragged to you about."

She didn't answer. She couldn't, with her mouth full. So he forgot about other foolishness for an all-too-short bite out of eternity, and they almost convinced themselves it was real as they came together that time.

Then Longarm got his breath back and sighed, "As I was saying. I wasn't the first in these parts to consider the obvious and drop it as too dumb to consider. Lawmen get in trouble that way a heap. You see, folks do such dumb things that you can't believe anyone could be that dumb, and waste time looking for some more sensible motive."

She sighed and said she'd been looking forward to owning even a small share of a land and cattle monopoly.

He shook his head and told her, "Never in a million years, at the rate they were taking quarter-section nibbles out of hundreds of open square miles. There's no way to grab small vital areas of fairly well-watered and nearly uniform short-grass prairie. Lord knows how Rathbone came up with such a loco notion. Albright and the other cowhands should have known it wouldn't work, dumb as they may have been, for a cowhand is a cowhand and anyone with sense to herd cows knows they herd most any old way in country such as this."

She said, "I told you Nat Rathbone had begun to have second thoughts and wasn't too happy with the way the locals were starting to react to the plan. He'd never expected a range war. He thought most homesteaders, given the choice of petty annoyances and selling out for a good price, would just sell out."

Longarm sighed and said, "King George and his redcoats figured the Minutemen at Lexington and Concord would just walk away from petty annoyances too. You *can* bully most folks and get away with it. But sooner or later somebody like Captain John Parker of Lexington or Jeff Wade of Elbert County seems to feel he's had enough."

She confided, "Nat was awfully worried about you too. I heard him telling that big blustering Duke Albright it would be insane to send anyone after you. They had quite an argument about you in the back room. I couldn't make out every word, but it seemed as if each was accusing the other of sending for those sinister Texas types."

He relit the cheroot and took a drag before he asked which one she had down as the importer of outside help.

She shrugged a bare shoulder in his armpit and replied, "Neither, to hear them both swear. I know Nat Rathbone took Duke and some of the others to view those embalmed badmen at the funeral parlor, and later he swore like crazy about them all being big liars. It seems they kept saying they didn't know any of those dead killers."

Longarm blew smoke out his nose and observed, "I'd hardly expect a cuss who knew a dead owlhoot rider to admit he did. But Diego Capaz wrote home about things getting rougher than planned and . . . Oh, Lord, how could any West-by-God-Virginia boy have been so stupid!"

She gasped. "You've figured out what's really been going on?"

He patted her bare rump and said, "Well, let's call it a way more logical possibility. That's what you have left when you eliminate the impossible, a possibility, see?"

Chapter 20

The Wades, Skinny Pryor, and the young white hand they'd hired to replace Diego Capaz had just finished breakfast as Longarm rode in from the county seat the next morning. But Miss Agatha still said he had to have some coffee and cake.

The two hands and both the Wade kids headed over to work on a brush dam in that branchwater Jeff Wade had reclaimed informally. So Longarm was alone with Jeff and his woman as he told them about Lawyer Rathbone having been the real brains, such as there had been, behind Duke Albright's swaggering ways. Even Agatha, having spent more time out on what homestead women called "The Big Lonely," could see Lawyer Rathbone had confused city lots with cattle spreads on the High Plains. Her husband snorted in disgust and said, "I told Sheriff Otis early on that we were dealing with a mess of total idiots. But he kept saying you had to have evidence to prove a stupid man made an untidy neighbor. Where do we go from here now, pard?"

Longarm said, "I got to go back to Denver. It looks like Albright and his top hands are gone for good. I'm still working on where Lawyer Rathbone wound up. Some wires I got back from Texas offer educated guesses about border badmen, but don't tell me who recruited 'em."

He washed down his last bite of marble cake and added, "I thought I'd try that old deserted Brandon homestead another time on my way back to Denver with that hired wagon and army mules out back. Could you have one of your hands run the roan I rode from town back to the livery for me?"

Jeff said he could do better than that. "Me and my boys will carry you as far as that Brandon place. Lest you find it not all that deserted. What are we looking for yonder?"

Longarm said, "Lawyer Rathbone. Now that I know Albright was only acting as Rathbone's pet baboon, he'd be the real owner of a spread with half a roof, well water, and no neighbors within miles."

Jeff whistled softly and said, "I follow your drift. What say we go get the boys, hitch up them Denver mules for you, and ride?"

Longarm waited until they were halfway across the barnyard to suggest, "Just get Skinny. He knows the layout of the Brandon place, and you'll want one grown man here with your wife and kids. I know how to hitch a wagon team, pard."

Jeff nodded, and headed due east as Longarm cut across to the pole corral and sod stable. By the time Jeff returned with the Arapaho breed, Longarm had his own saddle in the box of the wagon, the two mules hitched to the tongue, and both their saddles aboard the bay and blue roan he'd chosen for them. They didn't seem to mind.

The three of them headed out, joshing, with Longarm driving, Jeff to his right, and Skinny to his left. As they covered the ten miles or more, Longarm noticed more than one drift fence sort of reclining in the short-grass, busted posts and all. Jeff allowed he and the boys had been opening up their open range a tad since Duke Albright and his wire-happy crew had crawfished off somewhere.

It didn't seem to take as long this time. A ride always

seemed longer the first time, when you weren't sure where or when it might end.

They worked their way along that draw to the west of the rusted-out fence line. Then Longarm reined in and tethered his near mule to a cast-iron ground anchor. Jeff and Skinny tied up to his tailgate grips. Then all three of them moved up the grassy slope with their saddle guns, Longarm and Jeff armed with Winchesters while Skinny hung on to his older but ferocious and reliable Spencer .52 repeater.

As they worked their way in, Skinny offered to circle wide and cut the sly lawyer's line of retreat off.

Longarm shook his head and said, "Don't want to tell anyone we're out here. Make 'em guess."

Jeff said, "A man don't fort up ahint sod walls with the avowed intention of retreating across wide-open range."

Then he asked Longarm, "Why do you reckon he'd fort up out here to begin with? You've yet to explain what you have on him."

Longarm said honestly, "I don't have shit on anybody yet. Ain't even sure he's out here."

Then the wind shifted and he grimaced, adding, "He's out here."

Jeff sniffed and said, "Something dead surely is. Don't smell as sweet as a dead cow."

Longarm said, "It ain't. We got so's we could tell dead Rebs from dead Yanks after smelling enough. You are what you eat, and cows eat more flowers than us."

With Longarm in the lead, they worked their way in. It seemed unlikely anybody still alive would want to hole up behind those old sod walls. But Longarm still moved in low before he spotted the dapperly dressed but somewhat bloated form spread out in the weeds of another corner on its back.

The carrion crows had been at the eyes and gaping mouth, but you could see it was Lawyer Rathbone. Longarm leaned his Winchester against the near wall as he dropped to one knee, not to feel for a pulse but to go through some pockets.

As the others stood over him, watching, he muttered, "We can rule out suicide. Every pocket emptied and nary a weapon in sight."

Skinny said, "I follow your drift. Somebody must have lured him out here to his own property on some pretext, figuring nobody else would have any call to ride close enough to smell that awesome smell before time and the critters had made him tougher to identify."

Longarm shook his head and said, "I'd say I was *expected* to find this poor devil, Ekuskin. I can likely get you out of hanging if you want to turn state's evidence as a poor primitive led astray by wicked Ksiksinum."

Jess Wade gasped, "Are you serious, Custis? I can't believe this kid I practically raised from a papoose has been in cahoots with a secret outlaw boss all this time!"

Longarm smiled pleasantly enough at the breed, even as he was saying, "I can't believe heaps of things this noble savage or two-faced trash white has been telling me. As you must have just noticed, he volunteered to swing wide and expose himself to anyone in here with a gun. He knew there wasn't anyone alive out here. Just as he knew there was nobody at all the first time he led me here, to give the ones who drygulched Diego and Cindy a better chance against a fair tracker."

He nodded at Skinny. "You tore in wide open that time as well."

Skinny protested, "I was sore at them over Diego. So mayhaps I was acting wild and stupid. But have you forgotten I was the one who told you where Rathbone's office was, and then fired on one of the rascals as he was aiming at your back?"

Longarm made a wry face and said, "Bullshit. You were

171

only one of many, including Jeff here, who'd mentioned Lawyer Rathbone. You knew I'd ask *somebody* the way. So you volunteered to show me there. Then you fired that shot, at nobody, to warn your pal upstairs to hide. He chose a dumber course, and we know how that turned out. If he'd just ducked into one of those empty storerooms as you'd suggested, I'd have never guessed he was there."

Jeff Wade was asking something. As Longarm turned to answer, the chunky but quick-moving breed swung the Spencer up and pulled the trigger with its .52-caliber muzzle staring Longarm in the eye.

The hammer clicked like a kid's tin cricket as Jeff Wade wailed, "God damn it, no!" and swung his own Winchester up to blow Skinny sideways out the gaping front door with a round of .44-40 in his shattered skull.

In the stunned silence that followed, Longarm shook his head and then softly stated, "I wish you hadn't done that, Jeff. I was hoping to get more out of him."

Jeff gasped, "Have you been sipping laudanum neat? You almost got a bullet in your own head, twitting an Arapaho breed like that!"

Longarm replied, "Not hardly. One of the reasons the Spencer is still popular is that there's never been a repeater so simple for a man to load or unload. Whilst I was saddling his pony for him, I took the liberty of pulling his magazine tube, snapping it like a riding crop to empty it in the weeds, and shoving it back in the stock. I knew there'd be nobody else he'd want to shoot at. I'd been suspecting he was up to *something,* but I wasn't sure what, and you know what we say about giving a fool enough rope."

They both stepped out into the grassy yard to stare soberly down at old Skinny's oozing brains. Jeff asked if Longarm knew why Skinny had wanted Diego and that strange gal dead.

172

Longarm said, "I doubt he did. He couldn't have done it. I figure we've accounted for the hired guns who drygulched Diego and had some cruel fun with an innocent witness as an added bonus. I told Diego's kid sister they doubtless murdered him because he wanted to drop out of a game that was starting to get mean. He might have been killed to keep him from talking about what he and Skinny did the day of that unseasonable blizzard."

Jeff moved back to lounge in the doorway with his rifle as Longarm hunkered to go through the dead hand's pockets. Jeff asked what the two hired hands had been up to that snowy day.

Longarm rose empty-handed to say, "Trying to get me into a fight with Duke Albright. They only had to ride the short distance from the bunkhouse on your spread, as the storm was just starting, to pull posts from the soft greenup sod and pound them back, in a manner to make it look as if Albright's pal, Kansas Ferguson, had claimed a quarter section smack across a federal post road."

Jeff scowled down at the body in the grass between them. "You're not making sense. Custis. First you say Skinny was working on the sly with Albright and this other corpse out here, and now you're saying Skinny and Diego Capaz were trying to get one of Albright's pals in trouble with the law?"

Longarm shook his head and soberly replied, "Nope. Neither Duke Albright nor the city slicker *he* was in cahoots with knew a thing about half the funny tricks with fencing that was going on. Neither of them sent for those hired guns. Rathbone's secretary says, and I believe her, the two of them argued about who'd been stupid enough to hire outside help that only seemed to stir the law up. That one I shot it out with up in front of Rathbone's office had doubtless been told it would be safe to hide in an empty office building after dark. He never came out of Rathbone's actual office. He popped out

173

of one of the vacant rooms after Skinny tried to warn him I was coming, by shooting past me at the wood siding."

Jeff stared thoughtfully at the big Spencer in the grass near the dead youth's boots as he soberly stated, "I'm missing something. Why would Skinny, or some mastermind he was riding for, hire gunslicks to kill a federal badge and then save him from them, or at any rate refrain from gunning you himself when he had plenty of chances?"

Longarm smiled thinly and said, "You know the answer to that, old son. I was more valuable alive. Diego Capaz was the one those three killers were hired to kill, with me as an alibi witness for the ones who couldn't afford to let him live."

It got awfully quiet for a mighty long time. Then Jeff sighed and asked, "Are you saying what it sure seems you're saying, Custis?"

Longarm nodded. "I'm afraid so, Jeff. You were using me, just as you were using your friends and so-called enemies. I could overlook your showboat game with the Albright-Rathbone faction, them being as phoney and nobody getting all that hurt. But Diego Capaz sounds as if he'd been born with a conscience, and Cindy Fuller was a really pretty gal who'd placed herself under my protection."

Jeff sighed and said, "Nothing that happened to your gal was any of my doing, Custis. Can't we just let dead dogs lie and allow this breed kid must have gone loco now that it's all over?"

Longarm shook his head, and stepped away from the dead breed to plant his boot heels more solidly in the grass as he told his old pal not unkindly, "It ain't over, Jeff. It hurts like fire to say it, but I got to place you under arrest for ordering the murder of Diego Capaz and Nathan Rathbone inside. We can worry later about how you duped him into going along with some of the other dumb things the two of you conspired."

Jeff stared thoughtfully at the six-gun riding cross-draw on his old friend's left hip as he licked his lips and said, "I sure wish you could see your way clear to giving me just one break. I did save your life that time, remember?"

Longarm quietly answered, "I remember. That's how come I left my own Winchester leading against that wall inside. I figured an old pal deserved a break before it was asked of me."

So there it was, like a sidewinder writhing in the poker pot as they stared silently at one another. They both knew Jeff wasn't half as fast on the draw. On the other hand, Longarm would have to draw, aim, and fire in the time it would take a man with a Winchester in his hand to swing the muzzle up and fire at point-blank range. Jeff said, "I got a round in the chamber and this carbine cocks as you prime her."

Longarm said, "I know. If you don't aim to fight me, drop her and turn around so's I can cuff you. Out of respect to Agatha and the kids, I thought we'd just go on into Denver. We can make it a federal trial, seeing you had those kids murdered on a federal post road."

Jeff swung the muzzle of his Winchester up so fast that nobody could have drawn and fired ahead of him. But when he fired Longarm wasn't there anymore. He fired his six-gun more accurately from a full pace to his right, blowing Jeff Wade back inside the ruined soddy, then running around to cover his downed target through the gaping window opening above Lawyer Rathbone's body.

When he saw what he'd wrought, Longarm forked a long leg over the sun-silvered pine sill and rejoined his old pal inside, hunkering down beside the dying man with his smoking gun held politely as he murmured, "I'm sorry it had to turn out this way, Jeff."

"*You're* sorry?" his old pal croaked, with a smile that recalled happier days on the old Chisholm Trail.

Longarm gingerly parted the front of Jeff's hickory shirt, and tried not to sound girlish as he regarded the neat purple hole in Jeff's hairy chest, asking, "Anything in particular you want me to tell Agatha and the kids, Jeff?"

The man he'd just killed pleaded wistfully, "Do you have to tell 'em, Custis? Aggie was so proud when the boys said they meant to run me for sheriff this November. I never really meant no harm, Custis. I only wanted to be somebody important, like you."

Longarm didn't answer as he fished out a cheroot and lit it with his free left hand. It wasn't easy. By the time he had it going and asked Jeff if he'd like a last drag, his old friend was in no shape to answer ever again. So Longarm gently closed Jeff's eyes for him and muttered, "You son of a bitch. You're still trying to use me, ain't you?"

Chapter 21

A few days later, Longarm found himself literally on the carpet in the office of his boss, Marshal William Vail of the Denver District Court, although Longarm had sat down uninvited in the horsehair-padded leather chair across a cluttered desk from the older, shorter, and fatter Billy Vail.

As the banjo clock on one oak-paneled wall ticked off another ice age and the rise and fall of Rome at least, Billy Vail read Longarm's report another time, sucking on a cigar and emitting dragon puffs of disbelief from time to time.

Longarm had lit a much cheaper but much sweeter-smelling cheroot in self-defense by the time his boss lowered the pages old Henry out in the front office had graciously edited and typed up.

Vail let fly a vast cloud of pungent blue smoke and said, "I just don't know about you, Custis. You ask for a few days off to go help a pal erect a windmill, and then you stage the last act of *Hamlet,* with dead bodies all over the stage and not a one I ever sent you after!"

Longarm flicked tobacco ash on the carpet, seeing there was no ashtray provided for guests, and seeing that ash was said to keep down the carpet mites, before he mildly replied, "I didn't know what was going on until I got there. But look on the bright side, Boss. I could have put our own federal outfit to a heap of time, trouble, and needless expense if I hadn't talked Elbert County into treating it all as a local matter."

Vail cocked a bushy brow and dryly observed, "You must have really had a hard row to hoe, seeing this Sheriff Otis and most of that county courthouse gang will be up for re-election come November!"

Longarm smiled sheepishly and said, "Well, the people around Kiowa *had* been saying mean things about old Mike Otis, but he and his friends all treated me neighborly enough."

Vail said, "I'm not arguing about jurisdiction. Lord knows our federal courts are busy enough. I got some reservations about all the holes in this statement you made for the Elbert County grand jury and had Henry spell better for my weary old eyes."

He stared sharply enough across the desk at Longarm as he added, "Let's start with this .44-caliber hole punched in Jeff Wade's chest by a .52-caliber Spencer."

Longarm stared innocently out the window at the sunny streets of Denver as he softly replied, "I'm a tad disappointed in Doc Miller. I'd explained some of the minor objections to my overall theory to the satisfaction of everyone else. But it seems as if a dentist promoted to county coroner just can't resist the chance to perform a damned autopsy. The sheriff and district attorney agreed there was a dozen ways to account for that minor detail, had anyone but a prissy coroner wanted to."

Vail said flatly, "I don't care about you bullshitting Elbert County, seeing they seem to enjoy your bullshit. I want you to stop bullshitting *me*. I want to know what really happened, damn it!"

Longarm hesitated, taking a long drag on his cheroot. So his boss continued in a friendlier tone. "It's agreed that you were on your own time for those few days, and agreed that this sort of impossible statement was only meant as a courtesy to me and needn't be filed as any federal beeswax. So let's have the truth for a change."

Longarm flicked more ash on the carpet, ignoring Vail's warning frown, and said, "Seeing you put her that way, and seeing I'll have to deny what I'm about to tell you if it ever leaves this office, I reckon I'll begin at the beginning."

Vail said that was usually the best place to begin. So Longarm leaned back and said, "All that rolling prairie an easy market drive out of Denver was settled about the same way, by the same sorts, as soon as the Arapaho and South Cheyenne lost it fair and square by acting up all through the sixties. Elbert County's blessed by more than one sweet-water creek worth mapping, and like I told the Wades, you can drill shallow for water most anywhere out yonder."

"I know why you carted that windmill out yonder," Vail said, adding in a plaintive voice, "It sure gets complicated once you started cutting fences just to get there!"

Longarm frowned. "I'll never finish if you keep trying to run my story off the tracks. Just picture good cattle and marginal farming country, open for grazing or homesteading and settled rapidly but sort of sparsely by mostly dull and sober country folk."

Vail said, "I've been through Elbert and many a similar short-grass community. Ain't none of them worth writing home about as a rule."

Longarm nodded. "Wouldn't have been anything going on in Elbert County worth a paragraph a year in the *Post* if a slick-ass lawyer from back East hadn't noticed Denver and Pueblo seemed sort of cluttered with lawyers, and decided he'd do better in a county seat where cowboys and nesters were doubtless feuding and fussing all the time over fences and water rights."

Vail snorted, "He must have been reading more dime novels than Colorado law books. Country folks raise such country produce as they can on such land as they have to work with. It's a way one earns a living, not a Hindu caste system."

Longarm mildly asked, "Why are you explaining that to me, Boss? Lawyer Rathbone was the Eastern dude. He was naturally doing less legitimate business than regular country lawyers such as Will Thatcher, Esquire. So he noticed one client who'd come to him in need of some advice on a minor boundary dispute was a congenital bully and born failure called Duke Albright."

Vail nodded and said, "I see you let Albright off pretty lightly in this interesting work of fiction, old son."

Longarm shrugged and said, "I had to. He was an almost harmless asshole. Prone to pick pointless fights if he figured you'd back off, but ever ready to be talked out of killing you if you refused to run home to your mama. He was fairly convincing to most, since the average grown man doesn't get in one gunfight per lifetime. So he made a perfect front for Lawyer Rathbone's imperial plans. Or he would have, had Rathbone had the money his really stupid ambitions called for. He set up a land and cattle corporation, with Albright as the nominal boss, whilst he retained secret control. The strategy he had in mind required more money than he could lay hands on, even after his growing secret empire commenced to show some modest profit. So he went to my old pal Jeff Wade, an experienced cattleman anyone with access to the county clerk's records could admire as one hell of a High Plains success. He offered to cut Jeff in on the beef monopoly he had in mind. Remember, no laws had been busted so far, albeit what appeared to be a mushrooming cattle barony, owned and operated by a mean son of a bitch who strung bobwire across open range as a sort of hobby, had induced more than one smaller neighbor to sell out."

"Dumb way to amass land on the High Plains," Vail noted.

Before his boss could lecture him on the Homestead Act, Longarm went on. "Jeff Wade could see that. Before he came up with a slicker plan of his own, he likely pointed out how much cheaper it could be for a whole bunch of kith and kin to just claim a quarter section each for a modest filing fee. We'll never know some of the details now that so many of the plotters will never be able to testify. But suffice it to say that as Rathbone and his blustering group went on amassing land and cows by hook or crook, Jeff saw the chance to go into politics. His wife told me, not long before he died, how he'd always thought he might have made his own name as a lawman had things been a tad different."

Longarm blew a thoughtful smoke ring and continued. "Putting a logical train of thoughts in the skull of a dead man, Jeff must've seen the sheriff they already had was a decent enough cuss who kept law and order in a quiet part of the country without frightening the horses or making children cry. So Jeff agreed to back Rathbone's wild scheme. It was done so secretly, there was nothing on paper, and I needed the help of Miss Flo Redfern, Rathbone's hired help, to get Abe Heinz, here in Denver, to admit off the record that he'd known his associate Nat Rathbone was beholden to a stockman who needed to be let out of jail on a superior court writ."

Vail nodded his bullet head. "Abe Heinz is no bigger a crook than your average baby-raping lawyer. Get to the noisy stuff."

Longarm sighed. "I've gotten ahead of my story, thanks to the way you keep jumping in. Long before Skinny Pryor had to wire Lawyer Heinz for his jailed boss, Jeff had taken to sneering and jeering at Sheriff Otis because Otis couldn't do much about the senselessly annoying ways of Duke Albright, or prove Albright was in fact behind some of the meaner night riding."

Longarm took a deep breath, reminded Vail they were having a mighty private conversation, and said, "Jeff and his hired hands, Ekuskin Pryor and Diego Capaz, were the ones doing the downright illegal stunts with bobwire and matches. Since Sheriff Otis could hardly prove a suspect who hadn't done anything had done something, he could only sputter and fuss. Duke Albright, knowing he couldn't be charged with anything he had an alibi for, sputtered and fussed as his own ornery nature dictated. But then Diego Capaz found the game was getting too rich for his blood and wanted to drop out. He knew too much to let him just go home to Pueblo and gossip about 'em in Spanish. So Jeff sent for some part-time trail-herders and occasional killers he'd met up with in his own trail-herding days. As you can see in that report, the Texas Rangers finally managed to identify all three of the useless rascals for Elbert County so's they could be buried and forgotten."

Vail nodded. "None of 'em were ever wanted federal. How come Jeff Wade sent for you to come and build him that windmill if he was fixing to have one of his own hands drygulched?"

Longarm made a wry face. "I chided him about using me that way the last time we talked. Agatha Wade said Jeff liked me as much as I liked him. He knew I had a good Colorado rep, and so he wrote to me for help, telling more fibs about the way poor Otis simply couldn't cut the mustard. That got me to not only cut that fence Skinny and Diego strung across the road for a federal lawman to bitch about, but put me on the scene to alibi Jeff and Skinny as Diego and Lucinda Fuller were getting murdered by their secret pals. When I got sort of upset about that, Skinny deliberately led me on a wild-goose chase so's I'd fail to cut the killers' trail. But at least I found out what a handy hideout the deserted Brandon spread might make for anyone who knew it was not for sale or hire for a spell."

Vail said, "*I'd* have looked there, once I commenced suspecting a sneaky breed who'd already shown me about the property. Tell me how you got on to them."

Longarm said, "It wasn't easy. It was mostly that process of eliminating you taught me when I first come to work for you six or eight years back. You just keep eliminating notions that make no sense and folks who couldn't have done something until—"

"Don't explain the process of elimination to the teacher who taught you!" Vail shouted. "Get to what you eliminated!"

Longarm nodded. "First off, there were heaps of things only them three hired killers could have done, before they'd all three been eliminated one way or the other. Jeff didn't want *me* to get killed. When he saw he couldn't get them out of town discreetly, he knew *they* had to be killed. I killed one outside Rathbone's office by chance. Then Wade gunned that second one in the back and said he'd just saved me heroically in an election year. That left the sole survivor doubtless fuming in considerable confusion. So Jeff must have told Skinny to somehow get rid of him whilst he set up another alibi for himself."

Longarm studied the glowing tip of his cheroot as he morosely continued. "I'd like to think it was Skinny's grand notion, not an old pal's, to sucker that last gunslick into trying to kill me. The breed had never ridden herd with me, but he'd seen how tight I might track and it likely worried his mind."

He stuck the smoke back between his teeth and said, "Be that as it may, when the resulting excitement gave Jeff the chance to twit the frustrated sheriff into locking him up for his own good, Jeff saw the main chance he'd been waiting for. Having the literally ironclad alibi of a patent cell in the county jail, Jeff had Skinny lure Lawyer Rathbone out of town and simply butcher him like a hog. Then, with no Lawyer Rathbone there to say different, Skinny told old Duke

Albright his services were no longer required. Sheriff Otis had a flyer out on Albright and his top hands, until I talked him out of it. Seems needlessly confusing to haul a big bag of wind back before a grand jury to state whether he was paid off or scared off, seeing he left in either case so's it could look as if Jeff Wade had run off a dangerous cuss Sheriff Otis had been afraid to mess with."

Vail thought, nodded, and said, "He'd have likely won when he ran for sheriff in the fall, if he hadn't been too sneaky for his own good and tried to sucker a real lawman like you into helping him look so good!"

Longarm said, "I told him I felt sort of used and abused at the end. But he never allowed he was sorry, even as he lay dying."

Vail said, "I'd have been mighty pissed. So how come this statement to this county grand jury says you and your old pal Jeff, between you, figured out that Skinny Pryor had been secretly working for Lawyer Rathbone, that they'd had a falling out as you and Jeff were closing in, and that poor brave Jeff had been picked off by a desperate killer when you tracked him out to the Brandon place?"

Longarm shrugged. "Skinny had nobody in those parts to mourn him. If you were Miss Agatha, would you like to tell your two little kids their daddy had been a treacherous cuss Uncle Custis had been forced to shoot it out with?"

Billy Vail stared long and hard at Longarm before he quietly suggested, "The fact you'd once been good friends never influenced you at all, right?"

To which Longarm could only reply, "Damned right! What do you take me for, a sentimental cuss?"

Watch for

LONGARM AND THE TEXAS HIJACKERS

191st in the bold LONGARM series
from Jove

Coming in November!

A special offer for people who enjoy reading the best Westerns published today.

WESTERNS!

NO OBLIGATION

Mail the coupon below

To start your subscription and receive 2 FREE WESTERNS, fill out the coupon below and mail it today. We'll send your first shipment which includes 2 FREE BOOKS as soon as we receive it.

Mail To: **True Value Home Subscription Services, Inc. P.O. Box 5235**
120 Brighton Road, Clifton, New Jersey 07015-5235

YES! I want to start reviewing the very best Westerns being published today. Send me my first shipment of 6 Westerns for me to preview FREE for 10 days. If I decide to keep them, I'll pay for just 4 of the books at the low subscriber price of $2.75 each; a total $11.00 (a $21.00 value). Then each month I'll receive the 6 newest and best Westerns to preview Free for 10 days. If I'm not satisfied I may return them within 10 days and owe nothing. Otherwise I'll be billed at the special low subscriber rate of $2.75 each; a total of $16.50 (at least a $21.00 value) and save $4.50 off the publishers price. There are never any shipping, handling or other hidden charges. I understand I am under no obligation to purchase any number of books and I can cancel my subscription at any time, no questions asked. In any case the 2 FREE books are mine to keep.

Name _____

Street Address _____ Apt. No. _____

City _____ State _____ Zip Code _____

Telephone _____

Signature _____
(if under 18 parent or guardian must sign)

Terms and prices subject to change. Orders subject
to acceptance by True Value Home Subscription
Services. Inc.   11476-6